# RUBRICS AND RUNES

*A novel by*

**GILBERT LUIS R.CENTINA III**

Published in the United States by Centiramo Publishing, New York, NY
*www.centiramopublishing.com | info@centiramopublishing.com*

Art consultant: Janet Frances White
Book layout: Pierce Centina
Front cover image © Catherine Lucas/iStockphoto.com

ISBN-13: 978-1-7347256-5-0
ISBN-10: 1-7347256-5-6

Library of Congress Control Number: 2021932298

SECOND EDITION
2 4 6 8 10 12 14 16 18 20 19 | 17 15 13 11 9 7 5 3 1
MANUFACTURED IN THE UNITED STATES OF AMERICA

*To all believers:*
*Keep the faith.*
*When God seems asleep,*
*He is very much awake*

# ACKNOWLEDGMENT

*For your gift of life*
*For your gift of love*
*For your gift of truth*
*For your gift of justice*
*For your gift of humility*
*For your gift of courage*
*For your gift of peace*
*For your gift of joy*
*God of our graces,*
*All praise and thanksgiving*
*Belong to you.*

# ALSO BY GILBERT LUIS R. CENTINA III

*www.gilbertluisrcentinaiii.com*

# RUBRICS AND RUNES

www.centiramopublishing.com

# CHAPTER I

# The Collection Thieves

N THE DINING HALL OF THE FRIARS OF Extramuros, supper was ready. Opposite the reliquary, the big wall clock struck seven in the evening. Looking like royalty and dressed in a well-pressed native formal shirt, ready for Armageddon, Father Derovere Tiburron, local Prior of the house, aged fifty-one, ceremoniously opened his room. On the door was pasted a pink sticker that proclaimed boldly: "GIRLIE IS MY PRESIDENT." Beside the sign and secured with thumb tack and pink ribbon, a pink Girlie doll swayed with the slightest breeze coming from Azucar Bay.

The pink doll was bizarre, like a caricature from the pages of *MAD*; but Father Tiburron was jaundiced in favor of things pink, and the Lady Goddess of the Pink World represented to him the epitome of beauty. He looked at the doll lovingly, recalling who had given it to him. A Cabinet member of the revolutionary government, of which Father Tiburron was a fanatic admirer, handed it to him the afternoon His Grace, Archbishop Khoneimo, officiated at a wedding Mass. The minister's aide had slipped him an envelope. Opening it later in the privacy of his room, he found a blank check inside with specific instructions for him to purge his community of Hugo loyalist sentiments.

Father Tiburron checked his wrist watch. Stretching himself to his full height of five feet and ten inches, he solemnly walked toward the staircase, moving like a very important personage about to meet Destiny. He stopped before the telephone booth and glanced at the miniature blackboard for possible messages. None for him. All the messages were for only one friar: Father José Morán. Smirking, Father Tiburron pushed the white button above the blackboard.

A piercing sound filled the hallowed cloistered walls, bringing forth cassocked celibates from their heavenly contemplation and scaring back into hiding the cockroaches and other insects in the crevices of the unkempt corridors. Father Tiburron enjoyed ringing the bell. This was his moment, summoning his fellow friars, whom he secretly regarded his lowly subjects. He relished his exalted position, and the bell was the voice of God which every friar, regardless of race, talent, size and color must heed.

The Reverend Father Prior was about to push the button again when a Spanish friar, deeply tanned and grown fat at the expense of the Republic of Islas e Islotes whose poor people he despised, appeared and hissed into Father Tiburron's ear: *"Basta ya!* Enough already! Do you want to lose your right thumb?"

This was Father Flaco Gordo, aged sixty-four, deposed procurator and inactive parochial vicar.

◦◦◦

A monstrous but pathetic fossil of the colonial past, Father Gordo was the busybody of this religious community of nine friars. He was the biblical fig tree sprouting leaves but barren, unable to bear fruit. He was also the most obnoxious.

He complained about everything in the country: the food he devoured with gusto, the water he drank with relish and, most of all, the air he had difficulty breathing whenever someone impertinent pointed out to him the errors of his sweeping generalizations and his fallacies.

Those who knew him slightly might be intrigued by his exotic tales of sacrifice while he was a missionary in China, but others knew him better, having had the misfortune of living with him. They soon found out that he was not really a missionary but a mercenary.

He avoided assignments in far-flung places where he could be with the common people, preferring to be in the capital to hold the purse. Many wondered whether he was one reason the Chinese had renounced Christianity and taken up Communism.

His mornings in Extramuros were squandered by finding fault with his fellow friars and tearing them to pieces behind their backs. When there was no one or nothing he could despise, he plunged into depression. He took three straight hours of blissful siesta inside his air-conditioned room, and then later visited other houses of the Order within the capital. At each stop, he ranted against his fellow friars of Extramuros, taxing the patience of those obliged to listen. His list of grievances was longer than the Litany to the Blessed Virgin Mary, which Sister Escolapia de la Merced of the Confraternity of Our Lady of Consolation and Cincture took care to memorize by heart.

Truly, how mysterious is the Inscrutable's sense of humor! In Father Gordo's case, it was almost like a curse. Despite his heart trouble, his rheumatism, his gout, his difficulty in breathing, he lived on, durable, even deathless it seemed. No community in Spain wanted him, for he was such a parasite.

On this premise, he had been dispatched to the Republic of Islas e Islotes where people were hospitable to a fault and smiled even when abused. For some reason, Father Gordo had managed to survive, like a stubborn weed that chokes healthy green grass. In his old age, he was no inspiration to the younger friars. They thought him a good reason for sinning when they did not consider him a joke.

Father Gordo's reference to his finger momentarily unnerved Father Tiburron who looked at the older friar from head to foot. Father Tiburron was missing his right index finger. It was not quite clear how he had lost it, but it was a great source of insecurity for him.

Even while he was still a seminarian, not one had dared to ever mention it in his presence for any hint of curiosity about his missing finger on the part of his fellow students was met with dagger looks that could kill.

His mother's last name in the vernacular literally translated to thunder, whose frightening sound matched his explosive temper and intemperate language. His bullying behavior was something that none among his peers and subordinates wanted to mess around with in his seminary days. Retribution came fast and furious like lightning, and he would readily challenge anyone who dared to cross his path to a fist fight. Of course, no one among the seminarians had ever taken him up on his challenge, but they vented their annoyance by talking behind his back.

He studied theology in Spain, where his province had just started an ecclesiastical institute under the auspices of the Archdiocese of Valladolid. The province would eventually be given sole authority to administer the school only after many years of being under the watchful eyes of the archbishop there. At the time Fray Tiburron was attending school there, government authorities had not yet granted it official status to confer a civil degree, much to the detriment of its initial students, including Fray Tiburron who emerged from there without any recognized theological credentials to his name.

He would later come to blame this educational deficit as the main reason his nomination as bishop by Archbishop Khoneimo did not make it to the short list of three candidates or *ternus* submitted by the papal nuncio to the Vatican. To become a bishop was — no matter how quixotic it might have seemed to some of his confreres with whom he had shared his secret burning ambition — an impossible dream he had coveted all his life as a friar of one of the oldest religious Orders in the world.

Fray Tiburron was sent to Spain along with two other native students because, while in the university, he and his group could barely pass the subjects. They were always given removal exams because they had conditional grades in almost all their subjects.

But he endlessly complained to his superiors that the Dominicans, who ran the only royal and pontifical university in Islas e Islotes, were out to get him and his fellow seminarians because they were jealous of them, meaning his religious Order. This was his way of justifying why he was doing poorly in school.

He alleged that the Dominicans saw his religious Order as a rival to their uncontested claim of spreading superior education like no other institution of higher learning in the islands. Therefore, they did not want future leaders of other religious Orders to shine.

His superiors could not afford a setback in their drive for native vocations as they had lined up school projects that needed more priests to move forward. Declining vocations in Spain did not help. This made the decision to send him and his classmates to Spain a no-brainer.

Going to Spain was not his preference, but realizing that his departure for Spain was a done deal, he played the underdog card, saying it was "better to go to Spain to imbibe the real spirit of the Order and to really live the cloistered life."

Like the Dominicans, his religious Order also devoted itself to spreading learning, although its schools had struggled for recognition and name recall among the elite's spoiled children. Recognition finally came when they constructed a school in the middle of a newly developed enclave that only the shamelessly corrupt politicians and the military generals fond of Rolex watches and the obscenely *nouveau riche* with money to burn could afford.

The new village was situated in the periphery of the financial district of Islas e Islotes. The developer had wisely donated a piece of prime land to the religious Order to entice wealthy house hunters to give the new gated community a second look because a lot of people had initially viewed the place with trepidation as it used to sit in the middle of *cogon* land, where blady grass grew abundantly in wild abandon.

The developer was from *El País Vasco* who emigrated to Islas e Islotes and made a killing in real estate, specializing in the construction of high-end houses. He also invested in a food conglomerate that brewed Saint Michael pilsen beer, the country's number one brand. While still finding his way around his adopted country, he came to know the former Spanish friars of Extramuros, most of whom were Basques. He felt a special affinity to the friars, taking extreme pride in the fact that the friars who first Christianized Islas e Islotes were mostly Basques as well. The developer's decision to donate the land paid off. Soon, the gated neighborhood flourished as the moneyed tripped all over themselves to purchase lots where they constructed palatial Mediterranean-style houses. Hollywood location scouts came a-calling, and scenes of a blockbuster movie about the Vietnam war were shot there. The lead Hollywood actor used the school's swimming pool during breaks in the shooting.

The school became a plum assignment within the Vicariate. Father Tiburron was eyeing to be the rector of the school, but when the new offices were announced, he was assigned to Guadalupana Monastery, a run-down structure almost in ruins, ostensibly by virtue of his having come from the mission. The archdiocese had tapped his religious Order to renovate and administer the church for the next fifty years since it was the Order that built the church and the monastery during colonial times.

Father Morán was chosen as one of two native priests to manage the school in the gated village. This incensed Father

Tiburron no end for he considered everyone his junior a *mere* subordinate, who should wait at the end of the line for choice assignments. He fancied himself as the leader, *the* one who would eventually lead the Vicariate as its first native Vicar or even as the first Provincial of an all-native province whose establishment at the time was being contemplated and encouraged by the then father general himself, a Gringolander.

At first, he tried to court Father Morán and other younger priests to follow his lead. But the younger friars rebuffed him, especially Father Morán, an independent-minded writer who marched to the beat of his own drums and whose literary works had brought honor and recognition to the Order. From then on, it became Father Tiburron's main personal crusade to do everything in his power to make "these upstarts" pay for "being disrespectful." When it became abundantly clear to Father Tiburron that his chances of being elected Provincial in the all-native province were nil after the new province had been finally established, he opted to stay with the old province, and so did Father Morán and five other native priests. This development surprised and angered Father Tiburron even more for Father Morán would remain a thorn on his side.

Despite his four years of theological studies in Spain where he spoke nothing but Spanish except when he was with fellow native students, Father Tiburron's *castellano* was atrocious, and his thick accent made him incomprehensible when he spoke the language.

In the strict confines of pre-Vatican II days, Fray Tiburron's lack of an index finger would have disqualified him from being ordained a priest, but he made himself handy around the seminary, enough for his Spanish superiors to overlook his handicap. Since until that point in time he was the only seminarian who knew how to drive, he ran errands for them – and he would do just about anything to endear himself to them: from fetching fellow seminarians at the harbor when they returned to the capital by boat from the provinces at the end of summer to picking up prescription refills at the pharmacy to loading the seminary's provisions for the procurator. In short, he was their gofer.

Father Tiburron's vocation, however, did come close to being aborted when he was about to take his temporary vows of poverty, chastity and obedience. The formators met to decide if he should be allowed to profess. Two black votes were cast against his favor during the first votation.

It took two more votes before a compromise could be reached that allowed him to take the vows.

After his stint in Spain, he served for a few years as a missionary near Machu Picchu. He came back to Islas e Islotes with the grave voice of someone who exemplified the generally unfair criticism levelled against former slaves: that once freed from their shackles and given some form of authority, they behave far worse than their former masters in treating their fellow natives.

His temporary assignment in Extramuros, a parish whose parishioners were mostly English-speaking foreigners, forced him to speak English, something that public schoolchildren in Islas e Islotes were taught the moment they reached third grade up to the time they finished college. But facility of language – or love of the arts, for that matter – was never his forte so he chased after the perks that came with having conventual powers. Before his permanent assignment as Prior of Guadalupana Monastery, he was assigned to assist at Extramuros upon his return to the islands, where he proceeded to drive parishioners out of Sunday Masses with sermons where he mangled the Queen's English. The big drop in Sunday Mass collection became so noticeable that his superiors started looking into it. Some of the pious ladies, who comprised a big part of the congregation, confessed that they had found Father Tiburron's ill-prepared homilies garbled, their polite way of saying that they had understood none of the English words he uttered at Mass.

Back to Father Gordo, if this balding loathsome sexagenarian had been a native, Father Tiburron would have gladly broken his gold-rimmed eyeglasses; but Father Gordo was a Spaniard, no matter if he spoke the language of Fray Luis de León like a Portuguese sailor. All appointments made by the Regional Vicar in the Republic of Islas e Islotes had to be confirmed by the Father Provincial and Council in Madrid. Father Tiburron could not afford to offend any Spaniard.

Father Tiburron was not fazed by situations like this; he believed in tactical retreats. Making plain that he was not, by any means, surrendering his dignity, he retreated quietly. These favored friars were supposed to live together in a religious community to serve God, in harmony with one another. All had left the world to make it better. In the daily battle between God and Satan, Light and Darkness, Love and Selfishness, Good and Evil, Truth and Deception, Beauty and Ugliness, they were in the vanguard, spiritual bulwark of less hardy mortals.

Father Tiburron read the grace. His subjects responded by saying "Amen." Before Vatican II, the *Serotina* or evening prayers said for the deceased members and the benefactors of this particular religious Order used to be part of the schedule before supper as a matter of tradition. Some communities even said the *Serotina* according to a manual written purposely for the faithful observance of this long-held custom. But now, with no one wearing the religious habit, it had been scrapped with the rest of the evening prayers.

So be it. There was a place for every friar member of the community. Was every friar in his proper place?

To the right of Father Tiburron was a vacant chair. This was for Father Procopio Bolero, incorporated *de familia* into the mother Province of the Most Holy Name of the Infant Jesus to facilitate his studies. Tonight, he was out on an errand for the Institute owned by the Archdiocese of Extramuros, notorious for its staff of ex-religious men and women, messianic freeloaders of Liberation Theology exploiting the poor in God's name.

*"Ad majorem Dei gloriam,"* as the jesuitic Father Juan Bernardo would crow in all his jesuitical lectures.

Before he entered the seminary, name-dropper Procopio was a school dropout. One day, he heard Mass. "In the home of my Father," the priest read the Gospel, "there are many mansions…" For Procopio, this was enough. He packed his few belongings, sailed for Extramuros and found himself knocking on the seminary door.

The next chair was also vacant. Its rightful occupant was Father Rafael Merino, a native of Valladolid, Spain who had a Ph.D. in history. A scholar and a gentleman, Father Merino transcended the pettiness of the cloister by opening his mouth only when absolutely necessary. The last time he had spoken was six months ago, after visiting the room of a ninety-four year-old, bedridden friar. He had uttered four words: "Father Santos is dead." And he had not spoken since.

Tonight, Father Merino was out jogging in Manuel Piniar Park.

The next chair was vacant too. Its occupant, Father Angelito Mayo, was from Alimodian. He grew up in Iwaram City, then went to college in Patagonia. He had finished a computer course, but now found this useless. The Regional Vicar had told him early enough he was morally certain he did not need a computer.

Tonight, Father Mayo went out to see a sci-fi movie.

Father Gordo's seat was the next chair. The one next to Father Gordo's was also empty. This belonged to Father José Morán, a poet from Tinin-awan City who had won prizes for his verses and held five academic degrees.

The next chair was reserved for Fray Crescenciano Ferrer. A Japanese half-breed from Cape Bolinao, he was the only lay brother in the community.

Next to Fray Ferrer was the chair for Father Tirso Hernández, a distinguished historian from Zamora, Spain. He had been Father Master of both Father Mayo and Father Morán and also of numerous native friars during their novitiate period. His students now occupied top positions in the new province solely run by the natives. Father Hernández brought honor to the Spanish race. He had emancipated the native friars under his care by encouraging them to finish at least a civil degree. For his efforts, he was ignored by Spanish friars who thought that the Republic of Islas e Islotes was still a colony of Spain. Father Gordo openly belittled him.

Between Father Hernández and Father Tiburron at the round table sat Father Alypio Rubio, a gifted musician, versatile writer and excellent cook. Naturalized a citizen of the Republic of Islas e Islotes during the Hugo regime, he actually hailed from Leon, Spain and stood six feet tall. He excelled in economics. He replaced Father Gordo as procurator of the house when the friars threatened to mutiny because Father Gordo had deliberately withheld their monthly allowance of two hundred pesos. The round table had been Father Rubio's idea. But as time passed, he knew it was a failure. Some friars looked at their seats as prized possessions they could not easily give up. The round table did not bring them closer.

Father Gordo finished his soup and then helped himself to the salad and the canned tuna. Now, he was restless. He breathed deeply while massaging his chest and looking at the three empty chairs between him and the Prior, and then the empty ones between him (again!) and the lay brother. He felt surrounded by a wide gulf and realized his own terrible isolation.

The Prior knew what would happen next. He encouraged Father Gordo to make his next move by gazing pointedly at the empty chairs himself. Two of their occupants — Father Bolero and Father Mayo — Father Tiburron had always disliked, Not only were they not conversant in Spanish, they were also quite uncouth.

Father Merino was *merely* a member of the Extramuros Administration which President Hugo had created to preserve the historic character of the Extramuros neighborhood where the country was first founded by the *conquistadores*. Therefore, Father Merino was no better than a Hugo crony.

As for Father Morán, the man's name had come up in Father Tiburron's meeting with the Archbishop before whom the friar had unburdened his fears and anxieties. He worried about his third term as Prior. This would be against the constitutions of the Order. He was an overstaying Prior and faced the prospect of reverting to being a mere priest.

But the Archbishop had assured him, "Don't worry, Derovere, you will stay... but..."said the Archbishop as he clasped and unclasped his hands. "This friar Morán worries me. He has been telling people that he would rather sleep with a prostitute than go to the House of Archbishop Khoneimo; I have written him about his deliberate omission of my name in the canon during his Masses. So far, he has not answered. You must punish him, make his life miserable. Such impertinence! Harass him. Make him feel unwanted. I'll help you keep your post here."

*"Ubinam gentium sumus?"* Father Gordo crossed himself, *"Estos jóvenes!* During our time we had to turn over our keys to the friary to the Prior after the Angelus…"

Fray Ferrer recalled how he had nearly fallen from the tower while ringing the bell at Angelus had it not been for Father Jonas Garin who caught him. Then, after that, Father Garin left the Order.

Father Hernández continued eating.

Father Rubio lighted an expensive cigarette.

Wanting to smoke but unable to because of doctor's orders, Father Gordo coughed angrily and pushed his plate away. Then, his eyes lit up. He scanned the empty chair to his right.

"Last night," the unofficial newscaster of the community

announced, "I passed by the Gringolandia embassy to have a good laugh at the Hugo loyalists."

Turning to the Prior as though only they two possessed Eternal Life, he softly asked: "Guess who was there?" The friars waited.

Father Gordo drank noisily, scratched his back and chirped like a *maya costa*: "Morán!"

Father Rubio stopped smoking. Father Hernández dropped his fork.

"Yes, Tirso. Who else? When you were his Novice Master, did you encourage him to collect diplomas so that he could become another Marxist priest like D'Escoto or the Cardenal brothers? This time he wants Hugo back, imagine? Ridiculous! What kind of insanity is this?"

The busybody gulped his medication and continued, "It's profitable to be a loyalist. You can smoke imported cigarettes and wear alligator shoes."

Father Rubio felt alluded to because he wore alligator shoes and smoked imported cigarettes. Fray Ferrer stood up abruptly without excusing himself. He was going to watch his favorite TV show on the *Catholic Channel*. The monologue of Father Gordo vexed his spirit. As for Father Rubio, it was his deep dark secret that, voting for the first time in his life in the snap elections, he had voted for the Hugo-Chavezcu tandem of president and vice president.

Father Gordo rambled on: "The Hugos are thieves! *Thieves! Thieves! Thieves!* This morning I was in the palace. I saw such opulence! I heard Gringolandia Congressman Steven Solarium say that the frivolous lady — some say 'First Lady,' others say 'ex-First Lady' — has surpassed Marie Antoinette in ostentatious extravagance."

Father Hernández, the historian, winced. How well did he know that the republic during colonial times had been subsidized by the Spanish Crown. He thought the First Lady not frivolous but fabulous. The Cultural Center. The Heart Center. The International Convention Center. The Groceries on Wheels. The Metro Rail. All her projects.

"*La ignorancia,*" Father Hernández remembered the Spanish saying, "*es muy atrevida.*" Father Gordo, he thought, was an ignorant friar, "*tan claro como el sol.*

⁂

Father Gordo's kind impoverished any foreign country they went to, ostensibly as missionaries. He thought Father Gordo was a disgrace to the Spaniards and to Spain. A pity one could not select one's compatriot, just as one could not select one's relatives. It was no one's fault that Father Gordo was a Spaniard and that he was born in Spain.

"Morán," Father Gordo now loudly announced, "is a crazy dreamer. First the poor. Then the convicts at the national penitentiary. Then the prostitutes. Then the juvenile delinquents... and now...," hitting the table with a fist, "now he's working for the return of the Hugos! *Qué horror!* I wouldn't be surprised at all if he'll work next for the beatification of Evita Perón!"

Moved by his own eloquence, Father Gordo delivered his final verdict: "These spoiled brats should be spanked and shipped to Nuncamuere. Then this nation can be great again."

"With the Jesuits?" Father Hernández could not hold his peace anymore. Father Gordo glared at Father Hernández. He had lost his voice.

Father Tiburron was ecstatic. So Father Gordo was not an enemy after all! He might even be an ally. They might not agree what the common good was, but at least they could demolish their common enemies: Father Morán and his so-called Hugo loyalists.

"I must greet the bride and the groom," Father Tiburron broke the impending argument before it could go any further. Addressing Father Gordo, he said: "Even without me, the counting of the *collecta* will go ahead as scheduled."

Father Gordo gleefully anticipated his reward. Tonight, he would easily net two thousand five hundred pesos, safely stashed away. He had long coveted a Japanese camera on sale at Marcay's. "For the good of the province," he croaked, "the Prior of this house should be a native."

Father Hernández and Father Rubio looked at each other. They knew what Father Gordo meant. As he was skipping the wedding reception, Father Tiburron changed to a red Lacoste shirt and blue denim pants. He took off his black Prada shoes and donned a pair of white sneakers. As vice president of the local chapter of the Free Elections Movement during the snap elections, he held much power in that body and was even more influential than its chair, a colonel who was a closet member of the Movement for Army Reforms or MAR. The officer was not only a dummy, he was also a scared cat.

On orders of Archbishop Khoneimo, Father Tiburron had organized a zealous group of pious ladies who did nothing but talk against the Hugos before foreign journalists and self-appointed foreign observers. Three Marias led this distinguished group, code-named "Triumvirate."

Maria Magalona, a receptionist at the Azucar Bay Hotel, was to do nothing but wash the dirty linen of the Hugos before hotel guests, specifically the foreign ones. She introduced herself to them as a "not-so-distant" relative of the First Lady, winking mysteriously. Because she was exceptionally good-looking, it was easy to believe her. She told them the President was sick with systemic lupus erythematosus. She peddled secrets of the Hugo household, most of them fabricated.

She smelled like a whore but her listeners did not mind. They were more interested with her tales of the "profligate" lifestyle of the First Lady who, she said, used to borrow pairs of shoes from her mother when she was still a struggling relation in Peligro. A close friend of columnist Jaclyn Tomás, the flippant journalist who once wrote that Saint Paul had succeeded Saint Peter as pope, Maria Magalona was a restless soul. Like her columnist friend, she loved to flirt with military generals.

She lived alone in a condominium along Yentil Boulevard, having dismissed her maid who had written home that her mistress had strangled her baby, born out of wedlock, to death because it looked like one of the piglets kept by a general's wife in Sehcilavon, a town outside the capital known for its state-of-the-art abattoir.

Maria Borromeo was a chapter president of the Alpha Omega, a church group that built houses for the homeless. Religion and piety were her chief weapons. During the snap elections, she had dressed some girls as "nuns" to add drama to their accusations of election fraud and terrorism. During the macabre "Miracle of Dasma," the stage-managed street extravaganza of Archbishop Khoneimo and named after a stretch of highway in the capital, busloads of people were dropped off at street corners to clog up the thoroughfare in a show of people power to force the ouster of the Hugos. The "nuns" were very evident, carrying the images of Our Lady of Agoo, under the special guidance of Sister Cristina, in charge of the Home for Unwed Mothers and living patron saint of the communist rebels.

"Humble marriage," said Saint Augustine, "is better than proud virginity." Maria Borromeo had in her youth aspired to be a nun, but a lecherous priest who was her father confessor advised her not to. She was his secretary for forty years.

What flaming passions the walls of the rectory must have concealed! The irreligious relationship only ended in the death of the priest who during one of their trysts gave his last kick. That happened on the eve of the Dasma Extravaganza. The parishioners, thinking that their parish priest was a saint, deeply mourned his passing.

Maria Feliciano fronted for Father Tiburron in a thriving wedding video business that he secretly owned. Her husband was a contract worker in Saudi Arabia. She was a bed-hopper and used her wiles to seduce and later to blackmail people of consequence at the Gringolandia embassy.

She first came up with the idea of the wedding video business. What better way, she thought to herself, to exploit Father Tiburron's key positions as Prior at the monastery and parish priest of the church attached to the convent?

It was manna from heaven, allowing the business direct access to the captive audience of couples dying to get wed at the historic church when they came to the parish office for the required pre-marriage interview.

Below, in the lobby, Father Tiburron found Maria Feliciano patiently waiting for him. She was with the bride's brother who now handed him a thick envelope.

"What's this?" Father Tiburron asked, pretending ignorance. Her perfume was subdued. She had on a tight-fitting pink gown which, with her thick lashes that did not match her slanted eyes, highlighted her smooth dark skin. The overall effect of her garish getup made her look like a costumed clown.

"Thank you..."

After reminding Father Tiburron of the reception in the courtyard, the man disappeared. Father Tiburron and Maria Feliciano both entered the parish office.

"I've gotta go. It's an emergency! Explain to them."

"The Archbishop left after the first course. He brought with him the necessary documents."

"Is it located in a village?"

"Six houses away from Santi's."

"Was His Grace satisfied?"

"What better stipend could they give him?"

Father Tiburron opened his personal safe to deposit the envelope inside.

"That's ten grand."

"Okay, I'll give you five."

"Fifty-fifty?"

"As usual."

"You need a pink car?"

"I already have three pink cars. My brother is keeping them for me."

"Nothing else you need?"

"A beach house."

"I'll tell them that."

"As usual, fifty-fifty."

"One hundred percent. There. Can we can go skinny dipping?"

They both laughed obscenely.

Alone at last in the church patio, Father Tiburron listened to the laughter and the music from the courtyard, which the religious community rented out to the public for wedding receptions and other important events. Glasses clinked. They must be toasting the newlyweds, he thought. Outside, the security guard hailed him a cab.

Father Tiburron got in. He could hardly wait.

"The Gringolandia embassy," he instructed the driver.

# CHAPTER II

# Encampment

"FELLOW CITIZENS OF ISLAS E ISLOTES," Jessie, a law student at the state university, addressed the swelling crowd. "The evil forces of Gringolandia kidnapped our real President and shoved him in Nuncamuere where he is being kept against his will. Now, our country is being ruled by Gringolandia green card holders whose forebears, lest we forget, collaborated with the Enemy in the Second World War and founded the Doblerama, an army of traitors that served anti-Islas e Islotes interests, and the Filterama, a dreadful espionage ring that sent countless of our compatriots to death. Tinin-awan and Mampunay fell, but our patriots continued to resist the invaders, choosing death over treason. President Pacifico Hugo, then a very promising young bar topnotcher, fought for freedom. And now Gringo-landia has betrayed its staunchest ally…"

Delivered after the comedy skit of comedian Abnoy Bin-saya and midget action star Bling-bling, the speech stirred the people who exploded in ringing shouts of *"Hu-go! Hu-go! Hu-go forever!"* World War II veterans, remembering their war damage claims thrown into the wastebasket by the Gringolandia government, faced the Gringolandia embassy and heckled: "Gringolanders, go home!"

Matrons kissed their rosary beads and raised their appeal to the Gringolandia President half a world away: "Please, President Bedone, the usurper is a communist. Her husband was the real Kumander Santi. There are no bras or panties or shoes worth displaying in her pink closets, but dig around Hacienda Candelabra, and you will find many skeletons there. Bring back our President! Kidnapper!"

Kumander Santi was the known founder of the armed wing of the Communist Party of Islas e Islotes. It was rumored that he established the rebel army in the vast landholdings owned by the family of Madame Girlie Chichi Vda. de Almagro. But people within the intelligence community had long whispered that it was really opposition leader Berthold Almagro who had founded the rebel army to weaken the Hugo administration. He had planned to become president himself by exploiting the political chaos that he expected to ensue. But it never materialized because, among other things, President Hugo was a better tactician. He was widely acknowledged, even by the opposition, although grudgingly, to have better political instincts than all his political foes combined.

Young boys and girls danced and sang to the tune of duo Hajji and Florante's "Galunggong." Slum dwellers throughout this unhappy land had adopted this song as some sort of an anthem. The ditty was a dig at the pink government and a humorous paean to the local species of the blue mackerel scad, which was plentiful in the polluted and fetid waters surrounding the capital. It was the cheapest fish they could find in the wet markets. They fried it in coconut oil. Along with rice it was a popular dish among the poor.

⌘

During the campaign for the snap elections, then opposition candidate Girlie vowed that her first official act if and when elected to the presidency would be to lower the price of this lowly fish by fiat. But a few months into her revolutionary government, the prices of food and of other basic necessities kept going northward with Madame Girlie Chichi Vda. de Almagro seemingly paralyzed to do anything about it.

Her advisers were at a loss to explain away her ignorant belief that the "law" of supply and demand, as she understood it and blurted it out during the campaign, could be "repealed." But they finally mustered the courage to explain to her that this "law" did not in fact exist in the statute books but was rather a basic economic law which holds that market forces tend to have a mind all their own.

After that, no more mention was ever made again of her campaign promise to lower the price of *galunggong* with the stroke of a pen, not even once since she first stepped into the luxurious presidential palace after being swept into power by the confluence of events in the aftermath of the snap presidential elections in which President Hugo was accused of rigging the elections by foreign observers, goaded by the local opposition.

Seized by longing for their absent President, the multitude flashed the V-sign and lustily cheered a gigantic blow-up image of President Hugo guarded by a live unblinking Islas e Islotes eagle perched on top of a well-crafted bamboo trunk.

*"Hu-go! Hu-go! Hu-go forever!"*

The tumult reached a gaggle of foreign correspondents sipping coffee inside Taza de Toro, a favorite haunt of fixers, swindlers, snake oil salesmen, pederasts and pedophiles and child prostitutes.

Dressed in a Hugo T-shirt and casual jeans, her jet-black tresses braided with red, white and blue ribbons, Georgina studied Jessie, who stood above them, enumerating the crimes of Madame Girlie Chichi Vda. de Almagro: She had usurped the presidency of Islas e Islotes; ordered the release of top communist rebel detainees; abolished the parliament; nullified and voided the constitution; dismissed tenured civil servants; robbed prominent families through sequestration and pronounced them guilty by association of the crime of plunder; and persecuted all Hugo loyalists.

Georgina frowned. The speaker's profile disturbed her. He looked cool like a prince she had once met in Europe on a sunny day when the *Palacio Real* was thrown open for a day to the public, and she went and ran into a public appearance of the Crown Prince who obliquely complimented her looks, asking her along the rope line if she was related to the First Lady of Islas e Islotes.

"You look so much like her," he said.

Those were the good old days. She was then in high school at Montesini.

Montesini! The good old days!

Georgina shivered as she recalled how her former school was transformed into a center of anti-government activities overnight by Sister Bruhilda and her ilk. When opposition leader Berthold Almagro was fatally shot on the tarmac of the international airport in the nation's capital upon his return from exile in Gringolandia, it soon became the main preoccupation of the Montesini Sisters to sow hatred against the Hugos.

❦

Hating President Hugo was a status symbol. After Almagro's death, the Montesini Sisters organized rallies and demos against the government. Like the foolish virgins, they neglected their mission of spreading the Good News. Instead they became political activists. They dismissed their classes and herded the girls in their school uniform into anti-government rallies and demos. They invited foreign correspondents to cover the events. They secretly worked with the communist rebels and the military reformists to topple Hugo.

"Who were present at yesterday's rally at Uriarte Field?" asked Sister Bruhilda. She oftentimes reminded her class, lest they forget, that she was a bride of Christ. "Whatever we do inside this room," she had the habit of intoning, "should be done in the name of Christ." The girls were her students in her Physics class.

Everybody raised their right hand except Georgina, who secretly wondered how in the world could Christ have chosen Sister Bruhilda as one of his brides. The nun was overfed and had a face that only her own mother could love. She was a bully. She screamed at the girls even when asking the simplest question. She had a parrot that she seemed to love more than her students. She also had the habit of talking to her favorite cactus. As much as possible she ignored Georgina except when she wanted to bully her.

"Georgina!" the bride of Christ now yelled. "Why don't you want to get involved?"

"Sister, I'm very much involved," said Georgina.

"You didn't raise your hand!"

This was her chance to get even, Georgina thought. She sighed heavily and answered: "I didn't want to mar my beauty."

The whole class laughed.

"How dare you!" Sister Bruhilda was livid.

Georgina asked, "Sister, do you want to hear what Bum Demalo said during Berthold's death anniversary?"

"The truth, and nothing but the truth!"

"Nothing! That's what Bum Demalo said. He said nothing. Cross my heart, Sister. So help me, Christ."

Bum Demalo was a shadowy figure who had been with Berthold since the slain leader's early days as a young and ambitious politician. He was tasked to provide security to Berthold once he stepped out of the airport that day the opposition leader was shot dead. Lately he brought fear into the heart of the loyalist movement as he was suspected to be the head of the dreaded Pink Tiger, a private army which was believed to have close ties with Kumander Santi.

Sister Bruhilda promptly sent Georgina out of the room to wait for her in the ante-room of the principal's office. She gave the class a long quiz and led Georgina into her office. Sister Bruhilda was school principal of Montesini.

"Tell me," she demanded, "is there a family crisis? Are your parents separated? Is your father living with another woman? Is your mother having an affair? Are you on some kind of drugs or something?"

"Sister Bruhilda," Georgina tried to control herself, "please remember you're the principal of this school, not the head executioner."

"You're a problematic child," Sister Bruhilda sounded overly concerned.

"Nothing's wrong with me. I just happen not to idolize Berthold Almagro."

"I'm suspending you for three days," the nun ended the conversation and showed Georgina the door.

Georgina spent the three-day suspension sketching the President and the First Lady. She drew Hugo as the Strong One, father of all inhabitants of Islas e Islotes, emerging from a split bamboo trunk. She drew the First Lady as the Beautiful One, mother of all inhabitants of Islas e Islotes, stepping out of another split bamboo trunk. Then she wrote the First Lady. Because her parents lived and worked in London, she wrote, she had no friend. Would the First Lady be her friend and guardian? She hand carried her sketches and letter to the First Lady's social secretary.

After a week, Georgina was pleasantly suprised to receive an answer from the First Lady, in her own handwriting yet.

"There's much ugliness in life," the First Lady's letter read, "and it's refreshing to know that somewhere out there, someone as young and as innocent as you, can understand what the President and I are trying to do for our people. I'm your friend, Georgina. I'll always be your friend."

Graduation time came. Georgina was about to march for the commencement exercises when she was stopped by Sister Bruhilda. "You can't graduate. You failed in Physics."

Georgina left the cathedral, where the ceremonies were being held, humiliated and traumatized.

Her grandmother then sent her off to London to join her parents. She finished high school there.

⁂

"Are you crying?"someone was asking Georgina. It was the young man who had just finished speaking.

"I'm Jessie," he said. "I thought I saw you crying."

Georgina wiped her tears. Jessie was no fair-skinned prince. He had olive skin, and she liked him.

Jessie used to work as a junior protocol officer at the foreign ministry, placed there by an uncle who was the country's ambassador to Syria and later appointed by Hugo as foreign minister to defend his beleaguered government before the international community against allegations that he had stashed billions of dollars of hidden wealth overseas, among other corruption charges.

His claim to fame at the ministry, as his colleagues used to recall much to his chagrin, was in seating Iran and Iraq together at the same table at a palace function, a *faus pax* of unimaginable consequences to the future of any career officer in the diplomatic corps. Only the timely intervention of an eagle-eyed senior protocol officer had saved him — and the country — from extreme embarrassment.

Being an only child, he grew up in comfort, thanks to his mother's pharmaceutical company and his father's position as head of the Office of Tax Management in charge of a district that included the oldest Chinatown in the world.

Tax cheats would rather give his father a generous portion of the millions they owed in taxes than cough up the full amount to the government. Jessie hated his father and eschewed the lifestyle he led, financed by his Chinese connections. He hated him even more when he discovered that his father had a number of mistresses and had sired three boys with his favorite lover. Now it became clear to Jessie why his father had always been a distant figure, unreachable almost, paying him no attention that he craved for.

With the Hugos gone so was Jessie's position at the foreign ministry. He quickly enrolled himself to read law at the state university. That decision, after the loyalist period of his life, would lead to a position at the World Council in New York, where he unleashed his dumb resentment against his father whenever he came to visit him. He treated him with contempt and humiliated him in front of friends and relations by dropping the bomb of his father's corrupt relationship with Chinese businessmen back in the good old days, something that no respectable gentleman as his father saw himself would want revealed in any fashion.

"We'll start with the motorcade!" comedian Abnoy Binsaya announced. "We'll let this young lady here represent our First Lady, the Beauty in Exile."

Egged on by Jessie, Georgina did not protest.

⌘

Father Tiburron soon realized it was easier for a rich man to enter the kingdom of heaven than for a supposedly poor friar to spot another friar in a Hugo loyalist rally. He had spent hours walking back and forth from Avenida de Naciones Unidas to Gerard Manley Hopkins Library, and still no sign of Father Morán.

Returning to Belleview Plaza at 69th Street, he was accosted by an urchin who smiled knowingly, "Sir, girl?" Father Tiburron shook his head.

"Sir, boy?"

"Go away!" he yelled at the top of his lungs. "Or I'll call the police."

He cursed Father Morán for being absent at supper and Father Gordo for being such a busybody. But Father Gordo was almost always accurate about the whereabouts of missing friars. Father Morán must be somewhere around.

*"Hu-go! Hu-go! Hu-go still!"* Hugo loyalists flashed the V-sign back. Humanity spilled all over, from Avenida de Naciones Unidas as far as the Billton Hotel. Father Tiburron stood in front of Belleview Plaza where people dressed in Hugo T-shirts milled.

A heavyset woman, obviously suffering from some mental problems, was holding court on a street island. "Girlie is a know nothing," she said to no one in particular. A throng listened to her. "She keeps on sucking people's blood. She's a vampire."

Oblivious to those around her, she sat stolid as a sphinx.

*"Know-nothing Gir-lie! Vampire Gir-lie!"* the crowd responded.

A boy of twelve, who looked good enough to belong to any currently popular boy band, sat beside the woman, sketching a flying vampire. The boy showed his *magnum opus* to the woman who kissed him on the lips and cooed, "Darling, you want a hard-boiled egg? I'll buy you some. Where will the wedding be? At Honeymoon Inn? Will Hugo Junior stand as sponsor?"

Her listeners whistled the Islas e Islotes national anthem. The reluctant boy-groom ran away.

"This is the only thing she and her vice president want." She gave the crowd a dirty finger to finish her sentence.

"Me," she talked to herself, "I'm more beautiful than her." She winked at the crowd that roared in response.

*"Approved! Approved!"*

Curtsying, she flashed the V-sign. "Ladies and gentlemen, Hugo-Chavezcu!"

Father Tiburron bumped into the wheelchair of a limbless boy.

"Careful, careful," the woman warned. "Donated by the most beautiful First Lady in the world."

Surprised that she could speak English, Father Tiburron pulled out a crisp fifty-peso bill and handed it to her.

"My name's Anita. I'm not for sale," she spat at Father Tiburron who managed to duck in time.

"In the name of Girlie," Anita said, making the sign of the cross before the now trembling Father Tiburron, "and of Gringolandia Ambassador Arbacus and of Archbishop Khoneimo: *Hu-go still! Hu-go! Hu-go! Hu-go forever!*"

Then Anita was gone.

Father Tiburron went on with his search for Father Morán. He spotted Rio Della, the wife of singer Hajji, beside her parked Toyota Corolla.

Three cars away Leoncio de Rosca, a regular also-run in presidential elections, was rehearsing some kids on the now familiar Hugo chant and V-sign.

Father Tiburron thanked God he was not a Hugo loyalist. With his right index finger missing, he could never flash the V-sign.

Two women, both elderly, were conversing.

"I saw the First Lady wave her hand from the balcony. She was more beautiful than Greta Garbo."

"Bilario and Comdolezzo are traitors. Sooner or later, they'll pay for what they've done to the country."

Defense Minister Pablo Comdolezzo was a Hugo protégé. He became one after he was introduced to him by his first chief of staff at the palace who later had a falling out with the President as a result of intrigues sown by those around the Chief Executive.

Those who caused the irreparable rift between the President and his first chief of staff were intellectually less gifted men but nevertheless more adroit at political survival than Rafaelito Salazar, son of a sugar baron. A poet who wrote haikus, he never lost his noble character even in the face of unfair accusations against him by the President's trusted advisers who wanted him out so that they could replace him with their own man as "the little president."

It was a highly lucrative position for those who saw government service as a means to enrich themselves rather than to serve the people. The chief of staff was the first and last person daily seen by the President within his official family. He could retrieve any document from underneath a bottomless pile of paperwork that needed the President's signature and thus could pave the way for multi-million peso contracts to be paid immediately by the treasury. The amount of kickbacks a corrupt chief of staff could collect in less than a year was enough for him to retire and to spend the rest of his life in the lap of luxury.

Comdolezzo, a Harvard-trained lawyer, caught the eye of the President, despite Hugo's uneasy feelings about the former's divided loyalties between him and his resigned chief of staff. But over the years, those feelings somehow eased and then completely melted away because the President was impressed with the performance of Comdolezzo, first at tamping down on corruption at the notoriously graft-ridden customs bureau and later for showing a pair of *cojones* in fighting the raging communist insurgency after the establishment of a rebel army by Kumander Santi.

It was as defense chief after the snap elections that Comdolezzo turned against his benefactor "following my conscience." He teamed up with Lieutenant General Fidelito Bilario, the deputy head of the Army and the President's own distant cousin, to declare that they were supporting the Movement for Army Reforms (MAR) and demanding the resignation of the President.

As for Bilario, for far too long he had harbored the ambition of becoming Army chief but an overstaying general, also a cousin of the President and more trusted by the Hugos, stood in his way. He planned on using the highly visible position of being the top military brass in the land as a springboard to become president of the republic himself. The breakaway was his last chance at achieving this ambition, and he was not to be denied any second longer.

❦

"You know," another elderly woman exclaimed, "President Hugo wanted to give his best after the elections. That's why he stashed lots of money abroad. That's for us. And now this woman is going to sequester that, too. She's worse than Hitler!"

Most of the rallyists were uneducated slum dwellers and squatters and they blithely threw the comparison with Hitler around, which could be taken as offensive by those who had suffered the insufferable at the hands of the Nazis during the Holocaust. But too much watching documentary shows about Hitler on the *Chronicles Channel* had made them think that the new mandarins who showed no concern for the poor were the reincarnations of the evil genius himself.

Islas e Islotes may be the only country in the world where the term "squatters" had been institutionalized in all facets of social life, in the media, in the Church, in the halls of parliament, on the lips of every citizen. After the devastation of the Second World War, the capital became a magnet of mass human migration from the provinces as people were drawn to it by the popular mythology about city life created by the transistor radio. The capital was where the action is, where the impossible can become the possible if someone is willing to work for it. It was the message they seemed to have heard from listening to the radio commentators who were often given to hyperboles.

But their lofty dreams were dashed when their quest for fame and fortune clashed with the harsh reality that the roads in the capital were not paved with gold. Desperate to provide a roof over their heads, they set up shanties on every conceivable open space they could find, along river banks, along railroad tracks, in abandoned buildings, under bridges, on other people's vacant lots and even on cemetery plots.

They multiplied like rabbits and became a gold mine of votes for politicians who mined these votes during elections. Politicians cultivated their loyalty by giving them dole outs. They stood as sponsors at weddings and baptisms and paid for funeral expenses. And the Hugos were no exceptions, surpassing any politician in memory in their generosity toward the poor. They subsidized their groceries with the Groceries on Wheels program of the First Lady. They gave them free medicines and granted them free housing. But no matter how hard they tried at eradicating the squatter phenomenon, the vicious cycle was impossible to break. They just kept coming from every direction.

⁂

"Ladies," Father Tiburron butted in out of nowhere, "did you hear Mass last Sunday?"

"I'm now a member of the Children of God," the first woman said.

"I've become a Muslim like Princess Tarhata," the second woman said.

"I've stopped going to Mass," the third woman said. "I'd rather pray inside my bathroom."

"The hidden wealth must be returned to the people," Father Tiburron said. "It was stolen from the people."

"Who told you that?" the third woman leered in disgust. "Khoneimo? That anti-Christ!"

"Don't you read the papers?" Father Tiburron asked.

"We Hugo loyalists," the women chorused, "have stopped reading the papers. They publish nothing but lies."

Once more, Father Tiburron found himself alone in the crowd. The three old women left him, flashing the V-sign, chanting, *"Hu-go! Hu-go! Hu-go forever!"*

Father Tiburron walked past the Islas e Islotes Movement of Ping Vidal and Romy Viterbo; past the Youth Democratic Forum of Cesareo Zagala; past the tent of someone who proclaimed himself "the greatest philosopher in the world"; past squatters; past street vendors; past Metro Aides.

This was not a rally, Father Tiburron thought. This was an encampment! This was a purely loyalist invention. They had pitched camp here, night and day.

From the third floor of a residential building, washed-up actress Adele Kanaan and fly-by-night movie producer Yogi de Veyra showered on the loyalists below miniature photos of the President and the First Lady. Pedestrians in Dean Conant Worcester Square rushed to catch the bounty, reverently kissing the pictures like blessed *estampitas*, all the while mumbling unintelligible prayers. All to Father Tiburron's horror.

The crowd thickened. The motorcade started with the chant: *"Hu-go! Hu-go! Hu-go forever!"* Vehicles honked in the familiar Hugo staccato.

The lead motorcycle was driven by Ping Vidal, followed by a jeep that carried actresses Alona Abad and Elizabeth Lira. Between them sat midget actor Bling-bling and Muslim action superhero star Moammar Saddam.

Character actor Carlos Villa and movie villain Johnny Escudo rode a top-down car teeming with beautiful girls. Model Annie D'Amor was on a bicycle. Abnoy Binsaya drove a brand-new dirt bike.

Actors became a fixture at these rallies. Many of them had enjoyed unprecedented privileges during the time of the Hugos in power: tax breaks were given to movie producers, a film center was constructed to showcase the works of indie filmmakers, an ambitious international film festival was launched to attract top film talents from around the world and show business people were always invited to palace events to rub elbows with world leaders, super models, famous athletes, artists, musicians or Hollywood superstars.

But there was as well an ugly underbelly to these deliberate efforts at co-opting the artists. Long before China had thought of attempting to build the world's largest skyscrapers in just ninety days, the visionary — some would say frivolous — wife of President Hugo had overseen the construction of the cavernous Film Center, with its massive and impressive Roman columns, in less time. But the price to be paid in terms of human life was too high. In the rush to build the Film Center in time for the opening of the first international film festival to be held in the capital, part of the building collapsed, burying alive scores of construction workers.

To this day, no one has been jailed for that unconscionable but totally preventable disaster caused by brown-nosers at the public works ministry who could not speak truth to power for fear of losing their jobs. Reformist personalities within the Hugo administration had pointed a finger at the fair-haired deputy minister of the First Lady, Julio Zetineb, as the real culprit behind the unnecessary loss of precious lives.

He used his Stanford MBA to captivate the First Lady who, despite being the second most powerful person in Islas e Islotes, was still very much a little girl at heart who never dreamed that being crowned a local beauty queen in a satellite city of the capital region would eventually catapult her to being, for all intents and purposes, the co-president of Islas e Islotes. And in this calculated stab to be the brains behind the First Lady, Julio Zetineb succeeded in a big and profitable way.

Although the public works department was not his political preserve, he saw to it that he had his dirty fingers all over every Film Center project contract costing at least a million pesos. He was able to convince the First Lady that since the project was within the metropolis of which he was the deputy governor, among other graft-ridden government posts he held, he should be given veto power on everything that had to do with big contracts. Crooked contractors whose bids he approved had purchased sub-standard steel bars that experts blamed for the collapse, according to a token investigation.

⚜

On the night the Hugos were taken out of the palace by helicopters sent by Gringolandia to "rescue" the besieged residents and defenders of the seat of power against the onslaught of military rebel attacks, Julio Zetineb clung to the luggage of the First Lady containing multi-million dollars worth of cash and jewelry.

He knew that wherever the First Couple would end up that fateful night, they would need financial resources to continue the fight — indeed, to survive. By assigning himself the task of handling the important luggage, he assured himself a seat in one of the four choppers waiting on the spacious helipad within palace grounds to ferry the First Family to safety.

Gringolanders, having taken physical possession of the First Family and their entourage, initially told them that the capital was under communist attack from all directions. And that there was no safer place for them to go at that moment but the flagship, an aircraft carrier, of Gringolandia's Tenth Fleet, which earlier had been deployed off the coast of the capital from its forward base in Japan in view of the increasingly unstable political situation in the islands. But in mid-air, the lead chopper pilot received an order instructing his party to proceed to a little-used international airport one hundred and fifty miles northeast of the capital, where a Gringolandia military cargo plane was waiting.

The Hugos were not allowed to ask any questions and the curt reply if one was given by their Gringolander military escorts came politely but firmly: "I'm not authorized to talk about it, Sir." Or, "I'm not authorized to give confidential information, Ma'am."

At the taxiway of the airport, they could hardly see or hear anything, except for the blinking lights of the enormous aircraft and the thunderous roar of its engines. Then from the aircraft emerged the figure of a tall Gringolander in khaki uniform, an air force brigadier general whose rank they could tell easily by just looking at the glistening single star on his cap and epaulets. He walked briskly and directly toward the President and gave a snappy salute.

The President saluted back, although looking frail and haggard from four days of futile efforts to contain the military rebellion headed by Comdolezzo and Bilario. He gave the general a nod of recognition. In happier times, General George Nella was a familiar presence at palace functions celebrating his country's special friendship with Islas e Islotes.

"I'm here to fly you and your party to Nuncamuere, Sir.

On direct orders of the President of Gringolandia. And I'm really sorry, Sir, but those are my direct orders."

President Hugo remained silent while the rest of his group looked stunned and turned to the First Lady for direction. All she could manage to say was, "Everything's gonna be all right." No one else said a word as they stood there powerless. At that very moment, the massive beast of an aircraft before them had come to symbolize the most powerful country on earth that was about to swallow all of them into a life of unwilling and uncertain exile.

With those words from General Nella, a contingent of heavily armed air force personnel, hurriedly airlifted for the purpose from the flagship of the Tenth Fleet deployed on standby offshore, started loading the luggage of the Hugos and their entourage into the stomach of the big whale sitting on the tarmac ready for takeoff.

Julio Zetineb clung to the special luggage for dear life; it was his passport to freedom for he was seized with fear for his life if left behind to fend for himself. The military escorts, upon approval of General Nella, who knew Julio Zetineb as a jolly if glib fellow in the latter's glory days, let him hand carry the luggage to the back seat of the airplane.

⁂

The motorcade slowed down to allow the entry of three mardi gras tribes. They emerged from a side street, dancing to the rhythm of *"Hu-go! Hu-go! Hu-go forever!"*

The top-down jeep with Georgina and Jessie was about to speed up when jukebox queen Melinda Solis signaled every-body to stop while she led in the singing of "I Shall Return."

Soon, united by a common feeling of loss, the whole multitude sang the song, everyone raising both hands in the V-sign.

The song was never finished. Two gunshots were heard, triggering a great commotion. The lights on the streets and in surrounding buildings suddenly turned off.

In the ensuing stampede, Father Tiburron instinctively scampered toward Taza de Toro. Half an hour later, still shaken, he heard a woman telling another: "An impersonator at Jackson's shot a loyalist. The nurses at Islas e Islotes Hospital refused to admit the victim because their hospital, they said, is not a Hugo hospital. The priest has refused to bless the dying."

"Let's look for another priest," cried her companion.

Father Tiburron groped his way out of the coffee shop. He did not want to bless any dying Hugo loyalist, either. Outside, it was pitch dark. In his haste, the friar fell into a manhole.

Five loyalist kids helped him out. His sneakers were muddy and his wrists were bleeding. The friar reeked of urine and of human excrement.

"Careful," an old man warned Father Tiburron. "Loyalists to this lawless government are like Jews inside a Nazi concentration camp. We're treated like less than humans. When we die, priests refuse to bless us. They sequester everything. Corpses. God."

As Father Tiburron tried to regain his bearing on the curb side, he grew even more determined as Archbishop Khoneimo to come down hard on Father Morán. If he could prove to the religious community of Extramuros and other houses within the capital that Father Morán was up to no good with his blatant involvement with the loyalists, he could eliminate for good a potential native rival for the position of Vicar.

As a consequence of his own initiative, the possible exile of Father Morán to a remote post in the province would please Archbishop Khoneimo, Father Tiburron thought to himself. This, in turn, would pave the way for his name to be submitted again as a nominee for bishop. As required by canon law, the list of nominees has to be updated every three years because the Church wants to be prepared for any unexpected apostolic vacancies.

Archbishop Khoneimo knew that Father Tiburron stood no chance as a snowball in hell to become a bishop since he held no civil or ecclesiastical degree, but he wanted to keep him on a tight leash so he kept giving him the impression that he was his number one choice.

Although the code of canon law specifically states that a candidate for bishop should "hold a doctorate or at least a licentiate in sacred Scripture, theology or canon law," Archbishop Khoneimo found a way to include Father Tiburron as the code also states that the candidate at "least be well versed in these disciplines."

In the last nominating process, wherein respected members of the clergy were consulted in the strictest confidentiality, they roundly rejected Father Tiburron in favor of three more qualified candidates. They included his former classmate in the Dominican-run royal and pontifical university who obtained his doctorate in canon law in Rome and his licentiate in sacred Scripture in Jerusalem. The Vatican promptly appointed the canon lawyer and Bible scholar suffragan bishop.

Trying to shake off the drying cake of filth on parts of his cloth-ing, he started to walk aimlessly looking for a cab to take him back to the monastery. The smell of human excrement and of urine bothered him just a little bit for he had experienced of-fensive odors far worse before while helping his now deceased father tend to their small piggery in the province while he was in high school.

The piggery helped augment the family's meager income from the ten or so acres of rice land his father was cultivat-ing, an inheritance of his pious and simple mother who never failed to attend church every Sunday and every holy day of obligation.

It was on this rice farm where Derovere had lost his index finger — to a knife-weilding brother of a young maiden whom Derovere had stalked. About two miles away from his house was a river where housewives and their young daughters went to wash clothes and to take a bath in the pure and refreshing water. He took a fancy to the young woman about his age at the time, almost sixteen. He used to watch her surreptitiously from a bluff above the river as she retreated into the lush bush-es by the river bank to undress and change her clothes after a dip in the river. It was during one of these voyeuristic adven-tures that the only brother of the young woman chanced upon Derovere ogling his naked sister down below.

The brother took out a sharp jungle knife and rushed toward Derovere intent on teaching him a harsh lesson. He aimed for his fingers resting on a slab of flat rock, and Dero-vere's right index finger took a direct hit from the sharp knife. While frantically jamming his fingers up in the air to make sure none of them was severed, he quickly jumped up and ran as far as he could without even looking back at his assailant. He came home bleeding and feeling numb in his dangling index finger, and his parents anxiously took him to town after an herbal doctor had wrapped his shattered index finger with hibiscus leaves, which the *herbolario* had first heated over hot coals to release its curative properties. The municipal health officer feared gangrene could set in and decided to cut off the injured finger.

A mechanic neighbor taught him how to drive. Derovere Tiburron paid him back by renting his old pick-up truck to transport hogs and rice and other farm produce to the central market in the provincial capital where he found ready buyers for them.

A distant cousin had entered the seminary ahead of him and came home one summer to recruit him to join the monastery. Back in the seminary, the Spanish formators had put a plan in place to aggressively recruit vocations from the provinces. Even then, they had already realized that the future of the Church lay in the teeming millions of poor countries, not in Europe where secularism was taking hold. In this plan was enlisted every seminarian to spread the word about the Order among friends and relatives, even if it meant lowering the strict standards of acceptance to the seminary.

Father Morán decried this development, believing that this laxity engenders careerism which he thought starts when seminaries become "avian hoop houses," a line he used in one of his poems. Later on in their religious career, they fall into the trap of clericalism, a subject of another poem by Father Morán: *Clericalism is the cancer that afflicts / Some clergy and nuns / A praying mantis / That masticates its partner / While they are mating.*

Derovere Tiburron jumped at the first opportunity to go to the capital to escape the drudgery of farm work that had stalled his studies so that he was already twenty-two years old when he graduated high school. He entered the monastery shortly afterward. Nuns, his initial benefactors, financed his seminary expenses.

The blinding headlights from an oncoming cab cut short his reminiscence. He kicked a lamp post so hard with his right foot that he recoiled from the pain.

"This S.O.B. Morán will pay for this," he muttered to himself as he hailed the cab.

# CHAPTER III

# First Of May

FATHER MORÁN BOARDED THE METRO at Avenida de Naciones Unidas station. He had just come from his parents' house where he had advised them, both in their sixties, not to join the crowd of Hugo loyalists in front of the Gringolandia embassy. At least not today.

Father Gordo had told him that Madame Girlie Chichi Vda. de Almagro would address labor groups and cause-oriented organizations that day, the first of May being Labor Day.

Father Gordo had also bragged that the Hugo loyalists would be made to kiss the dust by Madame Girlie Chichi Vda. de Almagro's "my people," a favorite phrase she used in her public speeches that only hardened the suspicion held by neutral political observers that she was dividing the country into the pink crowd ("my people") on one hand and the Hugo loyalists ("sub-humans") on the other. Nothing in between.

It was enough to make Father Morán decide to get into the fray. He was thirty-three, but he still loved adventure. Sheltered in the monastery for so long, he ached to tell the world:

Here I am, a child of God. Not only that. I'm also a priest

forever, according to the Order of Melchizedek. I write poems. In my poetry, I speak of the destitute, the exiled, the oppressed. My heart is with the Hugo loyalists who are also children of God.

The back of Father Morán's T-shirt had the words: "GOT LEID IN THE ISLAND." The T-shirt was given to him by a Hugo loyalist. Walking past the skating rink at Piniar Park, the young friar heard footsteps behind him. Sensing danger, he quickened his pace and shortly found himself in the food kiosk of the deaf-mutes who were conversing in sign language. The stalker, it turned out, was a stocky middle-aged foreigner. He appeared without a neck, which was enveloped in folds of fat hanging around his chin, so that his head looked as though it was not at all connected by his neck to the rest of his body. Without any introduction, the stranger sat down beside the priest.

"Sonny," he asked, "you live around here?"

Father Morán nodded.

The stranger had trouble focusing his eyes. "I like your shirt. I like what it says on the back. We're not on the island, but I know of a very conducive place nearby."

Father Morán was not stupid.

"How much?" the stranger asked. Direct. To the point.

The deaf-mutes were not stupid, either. They started making what looked like obscene signs.

"I'm with the Hugo loyalists," the priest said. "Why don't you join us in protest against the Gringolandia government's tossing of our President in Nuncamuere?"

Bemused, the stranger abruptly stood up and left shaking his head.

❦

T.M. Kaluwalhatian Street overflowed with people, every square inch taken over by humanity.

There was Sister Bruhilda, self-appointed leader of the Girlie defenders, comporting herself as if she could personally decapitate all Hugo loyalists before judgment day. She was all over the place, bellowing instructions here and directions there, herding and pushing her Girlie wards, waddling like a duck. And she was looking ridiculous out of breath and sweating profusely in her layered religious habit under the oppressive heat of the tropical sun.

*"Hu-go! Hu-go! Hu-go forever!"*

*"Gir-lie! Gir-lie! Gir-lie! Gir-lie!"*

Hugo loyalists, statistically outnumbered, stood their ground, yelling and pushing back. Their territory had been cordoned. Anyone wishing to join them was shooed off. Sister Bruhilda scampered around, determined to whip her wards into a semblance of Archbishop Khoneimo's "people power" for foreign correspondents to take notice and for the whole world to applaud.

Father Morán pushed and shoved, forcing his way in.

A one-eyed man with foul breath came rushing forth, brandishing a gleaming machete in his right hand, shouting, "Where are the loyalists? I will behead them all."

Sister Bruhilda told her wards to make way for the man with the machete.

"There!" she pointed. "Off with their heads!"

"But why?" Father Morán asked a young woman in her school uniform.

"The Hugo loyalists plan to assassinate Girlie," the young

woman answered, her eyes blazing with fury. "We must strike first before they can make their move."

"But they are outnumbered. They are peacefully encamped."

"Megan Reynoso!" Sister Bruhilda screamed, arms akimbo. "Don't talk to strangers!"

Megan left Father Morán's side.

"People of God," Sister Bruhilda orchestrated the crowd, "all together now!"

*"Less than human! Abandonados! Hidden Wealth! Lupus Erythematosus! Abandonados!"*

The Hugo loyalists shouted back: *"Galunggong! Vampires! Usurpers!"*

Bum Demalo, the shadowy leader of the Pink Tiger, and his bodyguards Sid and Blah-blah were there, fully armed and fully secured by thugs with pink bands around their right arms. The thugs had stones and broken beer and soda bottles in their hands.

Anita and her disabled boy on the wheelchair were shouting. *"Gir-lie Know Nothing! Gir-lie Know Nothing!"*

*"Gir-lie Know Nothing!"* Anita was flashing the V-sign.

*"Hu-go! Hu-go! Hu-go forever!"* the boy was seconding her, also flashing the V-sign. Bum Demalo exchanged stern, annoyed glances with his two bodyguards. He started feeling for his gun. It was a signal for Sid and Blah-blah to do something.

Sid picked up a corn cob and hurled it at Anita. It hit the boy instead who ducked and fell from his wheelchair. "I'll report you to the First Lady," Anita wailed. "The wheelchair comes from her."

"Sequester the wheelchair!" Sister Bruhilda ordered, punching both ears of the boy. His nose was bloody from the fall.

Pandemonium broke loose. The sky darkened with stones and bottles.

Cries rose in the air. People turned to flee, leaving peanut stands, soup cauldrons and rubber slippers behind.

⁂

The *de facto* government of Madame Girlie Chichi Vda. de Almagro had become an occupation government. Hugo loyalists were being treated as the enemy to be hunted down and killed if necessary. Hundreds would be wounded that night and scores more would die and corpses would be found strewn behind the Central Bank, beside creeks, in grassy spots or floating in stinky *esteros*.

Father Morán found himself inside the first floor of the National Library together with a group of police officers and a ragtag band of Hugo loyalists.

Outside the gate, the hungry pink crowd demanded that Hugo loyalists give themselves up to avoid bloodshed.

"Do something!" Father Morán told a pious-looking colonel who was fingering his rosary beads.

"I can't," the colonel replied. "Orders from the boss."

"Boss? Which boss?"

"Bum Demalo."

The colonel stopped fingering his rosary. He turned to the wall and hit it with his right fist. He began to cry unabashedly.

A tall, dark man, both eyes blackened, rushed into the lobby followed by a pretty young woman in standard flaming red Hugo color. She looked fresh, unscathed. Seeing her, a young lieutenant nearby snatched a pink T-shirt from a vendor and locked the gate. The toothless vendor cursed him, denouncing military brutality.

"God!" the tall, dark man exclaimed, "there's a madman outside swinging a machete!" The young girl fell on the floor beside him. He introduced her to the people in the room, "This is my daughter. She was nearly hacked by the madman." The young lieutenant timidly approached father and daughter.

"Here," he said, "wear this pink T-shirt so I can bring you home." She glanced at him, tears in her eyes, looking very young and vulnerable.

"Never! Never! Never!" She burst into hysterics and pushed the pink T-shirt away.

Later, after having calmed down, the young woman gave her full name to the young officer: Tess Segismundo. She verbally gave him her address which he encrypted in his mind.

"Don't force her," Father Morán said to Lieutenant Marfori. He picked up the pink T-shirt and returned it to the officer.

"Who are you, anyway?" the young lieutenant asked.

"I'm a priest."

Silence took hold of the whole situation. Had a pin been dropped it would have sounded like a bomb.

"Let's go," the priest said. "Don't be afraid. Follow me."

The Hugo loyalists walked behind him like a flock of sheep following the shepherd.

"I'm a priest," Father Morán shouted at the pink crowd. "These are my companions. Make way for all of us. Officer, please unlock the gate."

The lieutenant grudgingly obeyed him. "Listen," he said to the young woman, "My name is Evans Marfori. I'm from Morolandia. Today's my birthday." She smiled at him and his eyes twinkled as he smiled back.

The crowd parted like the Red Sea for Father Morán and his companions to pass. As they turned at the corner, they sang "Happy Birthday."

⚜

Inside the Church of the Apostles compound, its gate locked and its vicinity guarded by eight men with high-powered firearms, Rudolph Rivera, a news reporter of *Islas e Islotes Express*, was talking to the sister-in-law of Monsignor Gustavo Ponderosa, pastor of the Church of the Apostles.

The pastor was not available. At that moment, he was taking his siesta in his air-conditioned room, oblivious of all the bloody maelstrom, having left explicit instructions to his sacristan not to be disturbed.

Menchu, the monsignor's sister-in-law, was a reporter who had crossed over to writing commissioned books. She was really from Almasag, her businessman father being quite infamous for some shrewd, barely legal business deals he had cut, but she married into a well-known family from Santaren, the Ponderosas who owned banks.

Soon after the election of Pacifico Hugo to the presidency, Menchu tried worming her way into the circle of Red Ladies around the First Lady, but she was not high enough on the social ladder to be accepted into the exclusive club. Stung by the rejection, she gravitated toward the opposition leader whose family took her to their bosom and gave her a sense of belonging. She became a newspaper reporter, writing forgettable reportage, biding her time, waiting for a break. When it came, it was huge.

The opposition leader paid her to do a hatchet job on the First Lady. Thus was born *I Told You So: What Else Is New?*

To drum up sales of her book, Menchu told gossip columnists that she faced arrest, harassment and all sorts of danger, but not a single hair on her head was touched.

When martial law came, she took off for London where she lived for many years running a highly successful recruitment agency and editing an anti-Hugo paper on the side. Now with Madame Girlie Chichi Vda. de Almagro in power, she had returned, riding the crest of victory, expecting rich rewards.

The melee of May first caught her by surprise while visiting her brother-in-law, the monsignor.

"What do you want?" she coldly addressed the beaten and bloody group that rocked the gate of the churchyard.

"The pastor! We need the help of the pastor!" Jessie shouted. Menchu took a side glance at Jessie. Not bad, she thought, not bad at all. Ah, but a Hugo loyalist! How could such a handsome hunk be so misguided?

"Please," Alona Abad writhed in pain, "let us in!" She had been kicked on the stomach by a fireman, one of many first responders ordered to the barricades to disperse the Hugo loyalists.

"There's a madman out there!" a boy volunteered.

"A baby has died," a woman announced.

"I'm the mother," another woman said, laughing dementedly. "Too bad I've only one baby," she laughed, "I could have offered all my babies for the return of Hugo. *Hu-go! Hu-go! Hu-go forever!*" She laughed and sobbed at the same time and flashed the V-sign. Menchu stepped back, gravely scandalized.

Georgina came coddling the dead baby, her Hugo T-shirt soaked in blood.

Horrified, Menchu turned her wrath on Alona and quizzed her.

"Aren't you the porn star? Why do you associate with this kind of losers? They're less than dogs. Repent! Ask forgiveness from Archbishop Khoneimo."

Georgina confronted Menchu. "Are you the maid? You talk too much. Call the pastor. We want to talk to him."

"He's sleeping and can't be disturbed," the sacristan announced in time to prevent a potential cat fight.

Monsignor Ponderosa was not far behind. He finally surfaced, very angry because his nap had been interrupted.

"My plants! My plants! Don't trample on my plants! Keep away, you scum!" he shouted at the Hugo loyalists. "What do you want?"

"The baby's dead," Georgina said. "We want it blessed."

*"Mierda!"* the monsignor cussed. Espying Alona he looked at her with lustful disdain. "Go to hell, you Hugo fanatics! You're no people to me. You're worms. You should be crushed!"

From the Areño Grandstand by Azucar Bay, Madame Girlie Chichi Vda. de Almagro's voice reached the battling groups. She spoke in a monotone as she reminded the people of the countless blessings she had brought back to the country. By deposing Hugo, she intoned, she had restored freedom and democracy. Then her supporters, as if on cue, broke into the singing of "The Internationale."

# CHAPTER IV

# Freedom Marchers

EVA MORÁN, MOTHER OF FATHER MORÁN, combed her graying hair before the broken mirror of the cramped living room that also functioned as a kitchen and dining room of the studio-type, two bedroom apartment she shared with her husband Jerry and three other children: Diego, aged forty, who was the eldest; Rose, aged twenty-six, who was the fourth; Isaias, aged twenty-five, who was the fifth. Ganymede, aged eighteen and the youngest, arrived the previous night from the seminary without saying a word. He was now occupying the steel-framed bed reserved for Rose in the other room, and Eva could hear him snore.

Cecilia, the third child aged thirty, got hitched with a serviceman in the Army's special forces when she was nineteen. She lived with her husband in faraway Nakatundan, an island stronghold of Muslim rebels and Al-Qaeda sympathizers. The last time Eva had heard about them, they already had four children. Christopher, aged twenty-two, the penultimate child in the family of seven children, was in Gringolandia working as a purchasing officer in a sporting goods store in Loverly

Hills. Father Morán was the second child, born seven years after Diego.

The apartment was located on Libya Street along Marmoset Drive, a working class neighborhood in the financial district across the fire station which had been renovated and painted pink after the departure of the Hugo administration.

Eva returned the comb inside the drawer of the other room, careful not to rouse Ganymede from his sleep. She lighted a candle beside the image of the Holy Infant enthroned on a small altar and flanked by a portrait of the exiled President on the right and a portrait of the exiled First Lady on the left.

Eva was a Bible Baptist until Father Morán embraced the religious life. Her mother Francisca was the pillar of the Bible Baptist community in Saracen, a village an hour away by bus from Tinin-awan, made a city during the incumbency of President Pacifico Hugo.

In those days Tinin-awan and its surrounding villages were predominantly Bible Baptist. The people looked down on the Roman Catholics who they thought worshipped graven images.

The parents of Eva settled in Saracen because her father Eliodoro maintained a farm there. He at the same time owned Maanyag, a sugarcane plantation, and Makusog, a coffee plantation near Mangkas, an adjacent town.

❧

The church bells were chiming when Father Morán was born. Francisca let the newborn touch the page of the family Bible, King James version, where Psalm 23 was printed. She wanted her grandchild to be a minister. Herself a philanthropist, she wished the baby to be a defender of the poor, the underdogs and the oppressed.

The child was showered with love, to the point of being spoiled, by Francisca. He poked fun at the teachers she had hired to teach in her Sunday school.

One day, a Roman Catholic priest visited Francisca and introduced himself as Padre Amen. He became a regular visitor and dined with the family when the occasion called for it. The family helped him construct his provisional chapel. She also bankrolled the purchase of the wooden images of the saints. The village folk did not really care about religion. They followed what Francisca and her husband Eliodoro told them to do because most of them were financially dependent on the couple whose love for people like them knew no bounds.

During the dedication of the village chapel under the advocation of *Nuestra Señora de la Paz*, the newly arrived priest baptized the seven-year-old José a Roman Catholic. Padre Amen himself acted as sponsor. Half the village found the solemn baptismal rites and, more importantly, the big *fiesta* that followed a welcome distraction in their otherwise drab existence. Soon, they too decided to convert to Roman Catholicism.

❦

Eva turned on the radio. Any time Father Morán would be arriving. She wanted Ganymede to be prepared before the priest arrived. Father Yen Karon, whose heart bypass surgery was financed by the First Lady before the forced exile of the Hugos, was on the air taunting the Hugo loyalists and calling them *abandonados* because, according to him, Pacifico Hugo had abandoned them. They had been abandoned, he said, by the devil incarnate. They must repent instead of gumming up the streets for his return. He then parroted what Archbishop Khoneimo had told foreign correspondents when they interviewed him at the archbishop's palace: The so-called Hugo loyalists were being paid to rally for the return of the Hugos. The movement was doomed to fail. What was conceived in sin would die in sin.

Eva switched stations. A woman block timer, speaking in a lilting accent, was urging all freedom-loving citizens of Islas e Islotes to join the freedom march. She then assured her listeners that the exiled President would come back soon.

"In the end," she said, "Good will triumph over Evil. President Hugo is not finished yet. His life is an epic. Every inhabitant of Islas e Islotes is Pacifico Hugo. Every inhabitant of these islands and islets is an exile in his own country."

Eva felt so forlorn. Her husband Jerry would soon be out with Diego, Rose and Isaias to join the freedom march while she had to stay put to look after their home away from home. Their apartment looked like a battle camp. Ganymede had stopped snoring.

Eva hazily snatched vignettes of the Second World War from what her memory could provide. "I can't marry you," she told Jerry, then a young sergeant. She had only finished elementary school when the war broke out and had dreamed of becoming a home economics teacher when it was over, although she was not sure when it was going to end. Many young swains had told her she was beautiful and sweet, charming and modest.

At the precise moment that she was turning down his proposal, a suspicious-looking character approached the gate of their antique house in Maanyag.

A servant warned that a member of the espionage ring had been sent by their neighbor Torribio to liquidate the whole family of Eliodoro and Francisca.

Torribio was a former *vaquero* of a kindly childless Spanish couple whose sugarcane plantation near Maanyag he inherited when they died in the sinking of RMS *Lusitania* by German torpedo in 1915. They undertook a voyage to Spain by way of New York and booked passage on the ill-fated luxury ocean liner. They had planned to meet up with some friends in England across the Atlantic before proceeding to Barcelona for a long-deserved vacation. Torribio had always coveted Maanyag even before the outbreak of the Second World War. Eva remembered everything.

An armed horseman was circling their property, sent by their sworn enemy Torribio who owned the plantation adjacent to their *hacienda*. Eva's elder brother, Eliodoro Jr., and Jerry had become close friends while stationed at Camp Barrett after their enlistment in the Army. That morning, Jerry was at his friend's house trying for the last time to get Eva to say "yes" to his marriage proposal. If that failed he wanted to bid them goodbye. He would continue the fight against the invaders in his home province across the strait that separated him from his own family in wartime.

Before the war, the elder Eliodoro and Torribio both had a gentleman's agreement. In exchange for Torribio's promise to give him a share of the profits from the sale of the next sugarcane harvest, Eliodoro had dispatched his laborers to plant sugarcane in the Spaniard's *hacienda* and to tend to the crop until it was ready for harvest. But when the sugarcane was about to be cut, Torribio conveniently reneged on their agreement. In anger, Eliodoro's son one evening took it upon himself to burn the entire sugarcane field, laying it to waste instead of letting Torribio get away with injustice.

Spanish *hacenderos* were remnants of Spanish colonial rule that had ended in Islas e Islotes fifty years earlier. A number of them, like Torribio, were originally *vaqueros* from Spain who emigrated to the islands, along with their masters. When Spain lost control of Islas e Islotes, their masters fled the country, leaving effective ownership of their lands to the *vaqueros* who seized the opportunity to better their own station in life. With their greed and lack of education, the former *vaqueros* soon forgot where they came from and turned out much worse than the people they had replaced.

Torribio greatly disturbed his neighbors on the eve of the Second World War when he proudly displayed Nazi flags in the balcony of his big house in his *hacienda*. He showed his true colors as a Nazi sympathizer when the Japanese invasion was in full swing, proclaiming his fealty to the Japanese Imperial Army and refusing to give any material aid to the defenders of Islas e Islotes who came for help.

Naturally, the burning of his plantation was a big financial setback for Torribio, and it quickly soured and ended his friendly relationship with Eliodoro. It was no secret that on his orders, the man on the horse, his right-hand man, came to start something very ugly. The horseman was circling Eliodoro's house with a rifle in one hand, hurling expletives at the family and threatening to shoot them.

Jerry challenged him to dismount. Before he knew it, he found himself jumping at the horseman and throwing him to the ground. The horseman tried to set himself free from the grip of Jerry who had easily disarmed him. He resorted to bit-ing the lower lip of Jerry, who profusely bled from the injury which would also leave him scarred for life.

Jerry grappled with Toribio's henchman who could not hold a candle to the newly minted sergeant, a competitive boxer in high school and highly skilled in the art of hand-to-hand combat that he had just learned from boot camp. After weakening his opponent's resistance with blows to his head and body, Jerry grabbed his own pistol and was about to pull the trigger when he heard someone shout, "Don't!"

The voice was that of Eva, Eliodoro's second child and oldest daughter. With the help of Jerry, they escaped in the nick of time from the possible carnage. Jerry was with them, his lips badly bitten by the henchman and still bleeding. He had saved them. That very day, Eva and Jerry were considered married.

⚭

Eva swatted a big spider which had started to spin cobwebs in one corner of the apartment.

For three generations, Eva thought, the Almagros from Tiyanak island had brought infamy upon Islas e Islotes. Berthold's grandfather was a military general who sold Islas e Islotes to the colonizers. His father founded the espionage ring for the invaders during the Second World War. His widow, Madame Girlie Chichi Vda. de Almagro, was a spider woman. She spun webs of destruction to entrap the inhabitants of Islas e Islotes with her gospel of hate. Like a poisonous spider, she secreted threads of venom as the foundation from which to build her house.

The noise created by the swat startled Ganymede. He peeped through the curtain separating the two rooms. His mother was crying. Ganymede was awake all night, pretending to be asleep by snoring loudly. Who could sleep inside a room with six other people who had nothing to discuss the whole night but the possible return of the exiled President?

"He's a great man," his father said.

"He's a hero," his mother said.

"He's the real president," Rose said.

"He was kidnapped," Isaias said.

Only Diego did not say anything.

"He will come back," they all said, including Diego who enthusiastically nodded his head in concordance with the rest.

"I didn't fight the war to bring the communists in," said his father.

"The woman is diabolical. She misrepresents Islas e Islotes and tests the faith of the believers," said his mother.

"She reads everything in her speeches, including 'thank you,'" said Rose. "She looks like a deer caught in the headlights without her teleprompters."

"She's like Medusa," Isaias said. "She turns whatever is beautiful to stone."

"Bring President Hugo back," Diego prayed aloud before the image of the Holy Infant.

Ganymede gathered from their conversations that Diego, Rose and Isaias were jobless. They blamed their misfortune — really, pretty much everything that was wrong with their lives — on Madame Girlie Chichi Vda. de Almagro. Rose was supposed to be working in Singapore, but she did not want to go back there anymore. She wanted to stay in Islas e Islotes and fight like their national heroine Ancilla Mistral, whose statue in Piniar Park would soon be replaced by that of Berthold Almagro's. Isaias was dismissed from his work in the Metro

Commission. Diego was the family secret that Ganymede had always kept from his fellow seminarians.

⁂

While teaching at De Chardin University, Diego met Teofilo Alma and within minutes, he became fast friends with the left-leaning Jesuit scholastic. His apartment in Patintero Road served as the unofficial headquarters of Masses Arise Movement, where Alma hosted informal meetings to expand the group's membership.

Diego's innocent association with Alma put him on the radar of the military. Intelligence agents picked him up along with Alma and separately incarcerated them in one of those fearsome military stockades that mushroomed around the country when President Hugo declared martial law, now lifted, fourteen years before. He was only released after he had suffered a nervous breakdown due to lack of sleep and torture. He was water boarded, the same technique employed against suspected terrorists in the War on Terror. His friend Alma died from torture in the stockade, becoming one more statistic among the countless activists who disappeared during martial law. Ganymede was too young then to know what really happened. He learned about it only from Cecilia who was vehemently against Hugo for what the military had done to their eldest brother.

⁂

The woman block timer was now crying over the radio. In her fifty-nine years of life, she claimed never to have witnessed the kind of callous disregard the lawless *de facto* government had shown toward tenured civil service servants who were let go just because they had served a now deposed President.

Ganymede could hear his mother crying with the woman block timer. He blinked his eyes in disbelief. His mother had never cared to listen to the radio before. His father had never talked about politics. His sister Rose had never gotten involved with the affairs of government. Now they were attuned to the latest political happenings in the country.

They finally exhausted the family forum on Hugo at four o'clock in the morning. They had taken the exile of Hugo as their own personal tragedy. Ganymede felt left out because no one had ever bothered to know why he did not want to go back to the seminary.

Why did his parents abandon their ancestral house in the province to rent an apartment here in the capital? They had told their children that their education was their top priority and that they needed to move to the capital to enroll them in the best schools their resources could afford, which was not possible had they remained in the province. But in reality, they had wanted to escape a creeping communist rebel presence in their area. Although their sugar and coffee fortunes had vanished decades earlier, leftist sympathizers in their village still viewed them as part and parcel of the oppressive landed gentry. Some landowners were targeted for assassination if they resisted rebel taxation. Ganymede stretched his body and pinched himself. Why was everybody in the family so concerned about the return of Hugo? He wanted to reassure himself that he was still in the same material world, that he had not entered another dimension.

To look fresh for his meeting with his brother priest, he

decided to take a shower. Ganymede did not know what to tell the priest who, to him, was more of a friend than a brother. To him he could say anything. The priest would never raise the red flag.

Four days ago, he sent a fake email to himself through a friend in the province who made it appear it was coming from his relatives there. With a real IP address from the province, the email was asking him to come home because his grandmother had died. He signed it with the complete name of his mother. The truth was, his grandparents had all died when he was still a baby.

The warm water from the shower excited Ganymede. His tumescence shrank when memories of his seminary days choked his senses. He entered the seminary because he wanted to be like his brother priest. He had heard him talk during his customary summer break about service to God being the highest form of chivalry. When Father Morán went to Peru to fulfill a vow to find God in the Amazon jungle, to seek the highest form of chivalry became Ganymede's search for the Holy Grail. He asked to be admitted to a minor seminary just when he was undergoing his pubescent stage as a teenager.

Their Prefect of Discipline, a venerable priest, was sent to Rome for further studies. He was replaced by Father Rembert Eclan, a newly ordained priest who was an exercise fanatic. He idolized Reynold Sketchers long before the muscle man's image was soiled by his messy divorce and his admission that he had used performance-enhancing anabolic steroids in his quest to stay on top of his game.

One Saturday, the seminary rector treated the seminarians to an excursion in Sunny Reef, a white beach fifty miles from the city. Ganymede was left behind because he had overslept and no one cared to wake him up. Father Rembert also stayed behind, having asked his assistant to go in his stead.

Father Rembert awakened Ganymede by playfully pinching his cheek. Ganymede rubbed his eyes and when he opened them, he saw Father Rembert in his exercise shorts, obviously proud of his hard-earned abs. The two had breakfast together, each enjoying a glass of lemon juice, a slice of wheat bread, yogurt, walnuts and a cup of coffee inside Father Rembert's office. The priest then led Ganymede to his exercise room where his dumbbells, abs enhancers, stationary bike, treadmill and other exercise equipment and paraphernalia vied for attention.

They spent the whole morning bantering and playing pranks like two little naughty children in the absence of their parents. The priest drove him to the mall where they saw an R-rated movie and bought popcorn, pizza and green tea for lunch. After the movie, they went back to the seminary. The priest let Ganymede use his bathroom for a quick shower.

The seminarian was soaping himself when the bathroom door automatically opened. Father Rembert materialized and feasted his eyes on Ganymede's young body, grinning from ear to ear like a solicitous fairy godfather. The priest stared at the part of Ganymede's anatomy which the boy was desperately trying to cover with his two hands.

"*Come on, Gani,*" the priest said, "there's only the two of us here, you and me, and we are both males. What are you ashamed of?"

The priest then proceeded to strip and slowly but teasingly covered his flailing nakedness. The seminarian, embarrassed by his own perceived inadequacy, hastily cut short his shower, quickly dressed himself and left bewildered, confused and frightened.

⹂⹂

A couple of days later, Father Rembert announced the presence of a dermatologist, a distant relative whose son was a senior high school seminarian under him, a classmate of Ganymede. He had asked the physician to perform a physical exam on every seminarian to look for any possible contagious skin diseases that he feared could spread since they were sharing the same living quarters and the same bathing facilities. As part of the physical education program of the seminary, Father Rembert had introduced wrestling.

But he soon started fretting that physical contact among seminarians during sports activities could increase the risk of contagion. He also raised the improbable and ridiculous specter that someone in the virginal group of teenage boys might be carrying some infectious diseases like HIV, the virus that causes AIDS. For effect the priest was fanning himself with a copy of a news magazine where AIDS was the cover story.

Like prisoners of war, the seminarians, after a two-hour siesta at three thirty in the afternoon, were herded into a cramped and dark hallway that connected the seminary to the chapel and were made to form a line, from the tallest to the shortest. An imposing statue of Jesus inscribed with the Latin words *Ego sum Via, Veritas et Vita* across its pedestal near the wide, double chapel doors seemed to look at the whole exercise with extreme disapproval, at least in the mind of Ganymede who kept wishing siesta had not yet ended so he could catch some more sleep.

The doctor ordered them to take off their clothes, including their underwear. It was not really necessary for them to totally strip naked but at the insistence of Father Rembert, the doctor readily agreed more out of concern to finish the job during the short period of time he was given to inspect every naked teenage boy than for any compelling medical reasons. He had already been handsomely paid for the job. Besides, he considered it a waste of time to argue a minor point with the priest who looked as eager as Father Rembert to gape at the seminarians in their nakedness.

The priest breathlessly watched as the physical exams unfolded, with the doctor yelling, "First on line!" With unblinking eyes staring intently, Father Rembert sat on a nearby chair which he had strategically positioned for an unimpeded view of all eighty-four high school seminarians. He admiringly ran his eyes on the body of each young man as the seminarians, one by one, submitted themselves to the humiliation of being publicly scrutinized.

The doctor examined them pore by pore, now with the assistance of Father Rembert who had volunteered to hand the doctor anything he needed from the medical exam kit: a pen light here, a pair of latex gloves there, a pair of scissors here, a swab of cotton there, a dab of skin ointment here and so on. Father Rembert realized how this act of selflessness on his part, at least as he justified it in his debased mind, could explain his hovering, and very uncomfortable, presence there among his wards.

To everybody's relief and to the complete satisfaction of Father Rembert, nobody was found with AIDS, a foregone conclusion given the fact that no blood test was ever ordered to seriously ferret out anyone who could possibly be infected. No one knew among the seminarians then that Father Rembert had concocted the totally bogus search for a possible AIDS-infected seminarian just to satisfy his perversion to have a close-up look at the sex organ of every seminarian under his care. It was Father Rembert's version of scoping the joint, so to speak, to choose the next victim most to his liking. It is a tactic employed by criminals who always make it a point to carefully scout their potential target before pouncing on it.

It was only many years after this lurid incident had occurred that Father Rembert's real motivation came into full view to everyone involved in that episode, except for Ganymede who had found out about it by accident much earlier.

One night, when everybody was expected to be asleep, Ganymede thought of stealthily grabbing a quick bite in the kitchen. The seminary worked like clockwork, and catchy phrases in large print such as **THERE'S A PLACE FOR EVERYTHING AND EVERYTHING IN ITS PLACE** were framed and hung on walls around the school to drive home this point. Schedules were imposed and expected to be followed — strictly.

At bedtime, no one was supposed to venture out of the dormitory or beyond the bathrooms without the knowledge of the Father Master. Stealing food in the refectory was certainly a punishable offense. If he got caught, he could be punished with menial chores for a week such as cleaning the four communal bathrooms, with as many as twelve shower stalls and twelve toilet cubicles in each one. And he would have to do all this by his lonesome self during his free time while the rest of the seminarians enjoyed themselves in their favorite pastime like playing basketball or a card game.

As additional punishment, depending on the mood of the Father Master and his two collegiate assistants, he could be made to kneel on a bed of sea salt on the hard cement floor with both his hands, each holding a stack of books, raised up to the height of his shoulders. He had to maintain that posture for as long as they thought necessary to plant in his head to always stay within the four wheels of community life: piety, study, apostolate and common life. Any activity that veered away from that imaginary wheel without the approval of the Father Master was considered an aberration. But Ganymede surrendered to his post-pubescent hunger and took the risk, anyway.

He was passing by the TV room when he heard strange, unusual sounds being emitted from the library. Curiosly, he peeped into the keyhole. The sight appalled him. By the light of the full moon reflected on the windowpanes, he saw Father Rembert and Ben Gurion, the dumbest seminarian in their class, wrestling on the floor, both stark naked, their bodies soaked in perspiration, their faces contorted in ecstasy. They were caterwauling like a pair of feral cats.

The following day, Ganymede went to Father Rembert's office with Rupert Arreza, their class president, who waved to the priest a printout of the email. Father Rembert hugged Ganymede to express his heartfelt condolences, whispering in his ear to come back as soon as possible.

❧

"Ganymede, hurry!" it was his brother priest calling. "We'll have ice cream in Hernando's Hideaway."

His brother, Ganymede observed, had changed a lot. He had become moody and impatient. He was slimmer now, his hair somewhat thinning, but his eyes were radiant.

"How are you doing?"

"As usual."

As if expecting something, the priest set the tone of the conversation from the very start. "We have the right to be happy, Ganymede. Everybody has the right to be human."

His brother had not really changed. He still enjoyed helping other people get out of the mess they had created for themselves. All the while he was not concerned about himself, or his health, or his own comfort – not at all. He was still the poorest friar he had ever seen. No one could hide the fact that he had the widest forehead one could imagine. He was always fighting for a cause, always looking at life as a game, where no one could ever lose, or ever win.

Ganymede took a teaspoonful of ice cream and smiled. He did not want to be a cry-baby. He would tell him he was leaving the seminary without being apologetic about it.

"I've got no vocation. Never had any."

"Congratulations! You deserve another scoop. One priest in the family is enough. I want my youngest brother to be a happy sinner, not a sad saint. God takes us for what we want to be."

"You're not disappointed with me?"

"By no means. You have your own life to live. Be there where you fit the most."

The priest switched the topic to the return of President Hugo.

*"Hu-go for-e-ver!"* Ganymede blurted out and flashed the V-sign.

Definitely, this Hugo madness had made of his brother a total stranger to him. He hated the Hugo loyalist movement for siphoning his brother's attention from him.

# CHAPTER V

# Second Coming

COMPLETING AN ISOSCELES TRIANGLE with Saavedra Zoo and Safe Environment Ark that did not admit adults unless they were accompanied by at least three children was Second Coming.

Formerly known as Mr. BIGS, the theater had been raided and padlocked seventy-seven times seven during the time of President Hugo for staging indecent live shows. It was closed for good the day the First Lady had the godless Soviet Union consecrated to Our Lady of Fatima.

A week after the Hugos had left, the theater resumed operations with a vengeance, this time under an entirely new management and a new name.

The religious leaders of Islas e Islotes did not raise a whimper of protest because Vita Marcelo, the new proprietress of Second Coming, was a cousin of Madame Girlie Chichi Vda. de Almagro and a generous benefactress of bishops, priests and nuns. A self-absorbed priest who called himself Father Nico was there to officiate at the blessing rites during the grand re-opening.

Two days after Ganymede had left the seminary, Father

Nico was still the Father Master known to everyone as Father Rembert. But now he had reinvented himself with a new name, or rather by using his middle name. For he was in fact christened as Rembert Monico Eclan, but he so loathed his middle name that he never used it. But now he had no choice in the wake of a sex abuse scandal in which he was at its vortex.

Father Rembert had lured a sick seminarian who was advised by the doctor not to skip his prescription medications if he wanted to leave for vacation on time. Father Rembert had enticed him to sleep in his room on the pretext that he, Father Rembert, could see to it that doctor's orders were followed. On the first night the young seminarian was in his room, Father Rembert lost no time in carrying out his evil plan. The seminarian was so repulsed by it and tried to resist as much as he could, but the fragile youth was no match to the muscular Father Rembert.

After the unspeakable incident, the seminarian was in a daze for days, walking around like a zombie. He had two elder brothers who were also enrolled in the same seminary aspiring for the priesthood. When they learned of the incident, they both wanted to kill Father Rembert and went straight to his room. They ganged up on him and beat him up almost to a pulp. Only the timely arrival of the assistant Prefect of Studies and some professed students saved Father Rembert's life. Thus ended Father Rembert's role as a seminary formator and started his new life as Father Nico at Calvario parish church where he was discreetly transferred.

All three Firenze brothers were expelled from the seminary despite their protestations. But all things considered, they also felt liberated for if truth be told, they were in the seminary only to please their mother.

The Assistant Prefect of Studies, in consultation with the Provincial and his counsellors, called their parents on the phone and asked them to come to the seminary to pick up their three boys. The boys, feeling the shame of sexual abuse at the hands of someone that their parents respected and with the encouragement of seminary authorities, did not have the heart to tell them the truth about what really happened. Instead, they blamed themselves before their parents for their expulsion by creating a story that squarely placed blame on themselves as the initiators of a rumble that caused injuries.

Their mother could not believe her sons were capable of such a horrible thing and was totally distraught, but her husband was relieved in his heart of hearts that for now, at least, he was assured that his genes would not end with his sons' generation.

Father Nico soon became the favorite spiritual adviser of Vita who adored his six-pack abs and kept inviting him to every event where some religious rite could be performed. To Vita, Father Nico was the forbidden apple she could not have and at the same time a spiritual clutch she could not do without.

The Tiples of Father Nico sang to add solemnity to the occasion. Menchu dignified the place by autographing copies of *I Told You So: What Else Is New?* Cackling, she announced she was writing a sequel to her best seller.

Vita Marcelo had benefited much from the Hugos. Her husband was awarded choice contracts. He was with the board of directors of several government-owned corporations. She was a Red Lady.

Sycophants of the former First Lady dressed themselves in red. They attached themselves to anything close to her heart in terms of her social programs for they knew that proximity to the wife of the President lent some cache to their name-dropping ways. It was a skill they had perfected to an art and kept in their back pockets to terrorize bureaucrats to do their bidding in favor of their shell businesses that existed solely to funnel kickbacks and bribes.

They were eager to implement her social programs because they enjoyed all the media attention. So they were there when the First Lady checked on the progress of a feeding program for poor children or when she visited the construction of new school buildings or when she distributed relief goods in times of devastating typhoons and other disasters.

Red was the color of the First Lady's dress when she first made her appearance in one of those heart-rending clips on the nightly television news. She was shown attending to the needs of earthquake-stricken victims of the capital early on in her husband's presidency. Someone suggested she looked regal in red and that they should all be wearing the exact same color when performing public acts of charity going forward.

When wild fires engulfed shanties in the slum districts every so often, they were there, too. It was being whispered around in this metropolis of swirling rumors that the First Lady herself had ordered the torching of those shanties to "beautify" the capital before any international event that she organized.

The rumor, of course, was just that — plain rumor, but it had enough legs to convince some gullible people to believe it and to pass it on as truth and nothing but the truth by means of innumerable spam emails, chain text messages and breath-less mobile phone calls.

And none of the Red Ladies parted their lips to quash it. As a matter of fact, they seemed to encourage people to believe it as it served their purpose of always giving the appearance that they were in the know about some well-guarded state secrets. This aura of possessing secrets deeply held by the Hugos enhanced their credential of being close to the First Couple. If perception is reality, these influence peddlers made sure that it was indeed the case.

⁂

Vita was exceedingly pious. She heard Mass every day. She did weekly penance by walking on her knees from the entrance of the church to the main altar. Her docility to the clergy was legendary. She was *hermana mayor* of many a church procession.

Before buying out Mr. BIGS, Vita had pledged, invoking the name of the Almighty, to donate one-third of the theater's income to the school which her niece, Megan Reynoso, was attending; one-third to her husband's alma mater; and the remaining one-third to Archbishop Khoneimo. Whatever income overlooked by the Office of Tax Management would go to her own major vices. Vita would have been willing to divest herself of all her material possessions and to donate everything to the Church, provided churchmen assured her without a doubt that, by doing so, she would directly enter the kingdom of heaven. But so far, no religious charlatan was willing to do so.

"The only things we really keep in life," the First Lady used to tell Vita and the rest of the Red Ladies, "are those we give away." Vita rivaled the generosity of the First Lady by donating a big chunk of her ill-gotten wealth to religious leaders. She did this to cover up for many things.

Vita's major vice was men. She got attracted to every man she was acquainted with. Her lust for men was equaled only by her longing to be saved from eternal damnation. What is hell for Vita but repression of her lustful desire? She secretly envisioned heaven not as a state of mind, but a paradise where she had all the freedom to pleasure and be pleasured by male elects.

Since her husband could never satisfy her sexual needs, she turned to sex toys for comfort, but even these could not fully satiate her cravings. Her money bought her all the men she wanted. There were always starving studs available, willing and able, as long as they were paid. One passing fancy turned out to be a blackmailer. Vita ran to the First Lady for succor and told her it was better for her to die than be exposed before the eyes of the world. The First Lady instructed the chief of her military escorts to refer the blackmail threat to the justice department. Vita's problem went away when non-uniformed agents of the Presidential Guards paid the man a visit at his apartment and asked him to return every incriminating love note that Vita had sent him. The man complied and promised that he would never bother Vita ever again for he knew full well that they meant serious business. But Vita never quite succeeded in exorcising herself of her sexual demons. She started having the recurring fantasy of ravishing the two angels with the flaming swords keeping watch east of Eden, before the august audience of judges, kings, prophets and other personages of the Old Testament.

When her relative Madame Girlie Chichi Vda. de Almagro usurped the presidency, Vita was one of the original turncoats.

"Did you visit your best friends, the Hugos?" a pilot who knew her many times in the biblical sense asked her half in jest and half in spite loud enough for everyone to hear in one of the parties she hosted to toast the "air of freedom" under the new regime.

"Who? Those thieves?" she snapped at him dismissively.

※

An intoxicated Ganymede Morán motioned to the waiter of Second Coming to give him another bottle of beer. He lighted another cigarette as he groggily stared at the twelve empty bottles of beer that seemed to be staring back at him like the Twelve Apostles in the painting of Salvador Dalí. The thirteenth order came. Ganymede gulped the beer directly from the bottle. He wanted it that way. It made him look tough and feel mature.

People around him abruptly dropped anything that they were doing and suddenly became hushed. Everybody was open-mouthed as a singing brunette, clad in a topless bikini, glided in, urging everybody to wave a pink ribbon at the old oak tree if they still wanted her. There was no oak tree around, so people instead knotted a pink ribbon around their heads and urged her to get rid of the bikini.

Four more brunettes, naked as the day they were born, took a vow, gyrating their hips and hopping from table to table. For five pesos, the audience could fondle their bodies. The first brunette threw all caution to the wind. Naked like her companions, she went straight to Ganymede. The woman tongued the youth's lips but received no response. Ganymede had passed out. She looked around her. Nobody was looking at their direction. She knelt and unzipped Ganymede's fly. Then she whistled.

A small boy of about twelve years of age wearing a pink Berthold Almagro T-shirt came from behind and reached for Ganymede's wallet.

Brunette number one was at another table, fondled and mashed by the audience willing to pay for the privilege of pleasuring and of being pleasured in return.

As the scene turned wilder, the crowd grew rowdy and insane.

The pink room of Second Coming was lighted like day. Everything inside was pink, except for the one-way mirror and the portrait of Madame Girlie Chichi Vda. de Almagro which was in all colors of the rainbow. She was portrayed flashing the pink sign, grinning like a goblin. During the snap presidential elections, pink was the official color she had chosen to differentiate her campaign from that of President Hugo who wore red, white and blue in all his reelection blitz appearances.

This obsession for anything pink and for anything red, white and blue by these two opposing camps was a bonanza for print makers and other suppliers of campaign accoutrements. It also artificially spiked the country's gross domestic product and caused a tremendous migraine headache to the country's economic managers who feared a runaway inflation and a gnawing budget deficit would ensue when the insanity was over. But having stayed in power for so long, the President and the First Lady only wanted to hear what they wanted to hear. His economic managers were therefore resigned to the fact that the snap elections were a necessary evil. Although President Hugo had four more years left in his latest six-year term, he was pressured into calling the snap elections to prove to Gringolandia that he still had the mandate of the people. Candidate Girlie, on the other hand, could not care less as her campaign was heavily funded by outside sources, the usual suspects with vested interests in the outcome of the presidential elections.

Tonight, Vita was dressed in a pink kimono. She wore a pink wig that accented her obesity, looking decadent. Since the Hugos left, she had bloated to two hundred thirty-five pounds. No slimming clinic could bring her weight down. Her pilates and her yoga instructors had each pronounced her case hopeless. Lately, her lust had been matched only by her gluttony. She was afraid to go to the doctor for fear that he might confirm her own suspicion that she was suffering from elephantiasis.

Among the pink crowd, however, Vita was the epitome of beauty. She was not only lascivious but also generous, so men who serviced her found her beautiful. To the Pink Ladies, she was no threat, so she was beautiful.

"Don't worry. You should be glad that you're no Marie Antoinette," Sister Bruhilda consoled her when she handed her their school's monthly share from the income generated by Second Coming. Vita was not convinced. She had always aspired to being compared to Marie Antoinette, and now Sister Bruhilda had doused her aspiration.

"I have a brilliant idea," the nun said. "I'll ask Dikdik Nognog to write in her gossip column that the deposed First

Lady is rumored to have bloated to pitiful proportion due to overeating."

Vita held her peace. She found the nun's proposal ridiculous. Nuns like Sister Bruhilda, whom she frowned upon, could at times think no better than silly girls.

*

Seated on a peacock chair, Vita scanned the one-way mirror and mentally estimated the number of patrons who could afford to pay one hundred and fifty pesos for tonight's live show special. There were exactly two hundred spectators. Through the mirror she watched two bouncers convert the sofa into a double bed.

The female performer walked in, dressed in a school uniform, her hair braided to enhance her innocence, catching the full attention of everyone. The male performer, dressed as a sailor, soon followed.

He was browsing over an old issue of a hard-core magazine that he had bought on sale at the underpass on his way to work. Both performers studied each other, their eyes locked in raging passion as the disc jockey started playing the anthem of the pink horde on the turntable.

The make-believe sailor mechanically kissed the make-believe school girl. The audience threw peso bills of different denominations at the couple as they moved from table to table contorted in different sexual positions. Teenagers threw coins and unzipped their pants.

*

Someone knocked on the pink door of the pink room. Vita

jumped out of her peacock throne. She pulled a string that dropped a thick pink curtain, fully covering the mirror. She went to the altar of *Nuestra Señora de la Regla* and lighted three pink candles. The pink room at once looked decent. It was suddenly converted into an office of the Pink Tiger, a secret organization out to eliminate Hugo loyalists from the face of the earth.

Vita opened the door. She was greeted by the sight of a drunken Ganymede being collared and dragged by the penthouse bouncer.

"Ma'am," complained the bouncer, "this juvenile delinquent occupied a table, ate one whole fried chicken and three bags of salted peanuts, smoked a pack of imported cigarettes, got lushed on thirteen bottles of beer and refused to pay the bill. Not only that, he kept on flashing the V-sign to every patron's annoyance. He claims to have been robbed. Shall we have him salvaged? Must be one of those squatters paid to attend loyalist rallies."

In this unhappy republic, salvage was a euphemism for getting rid of people with a single bullet to their head or with as many bullets as the trigger-happy paid assassin would wish to dispense out of the bullet chamber.

Vita's gaze fell upon the boy's unzipped fly. Her feeling of anger was replaced by lust.

"No, leave him to me. I know how to deal with his kind."

It was pitch dark. He was running naked, pursued by Father Rembert Eclan. The globe was straddled by a witch, who had made the people mad after forcing them to drink from a well. He did not want to lose his mind like them so he refused to drink the water from the well. Voices jeered at him.

"He's mad!"

He ran as fast as he could.

"He's mad!"

He ran inside a church, which was painted pink. The pews were empty. The images of the saints, solemn and grave, were deserting the church one by one. They were forming a queue from the nave to the entrance of the church. Archbishop Khoneimo was driving the saints out of the church.

"So you refuse to drink the water? Get out of here! You're all mad!"

He ran to the nearest police station. The wives of the police officers were ululating in grief as their husbands had been gelded by the witch. The whole metropolis was in a state of anarchy. The Hugo loyalists had been turned to stone! He kept running. Fingers were playing all over his body.

"Drink the water, so you'll keep your sanity like the rest of us!"

"He doesn't want to drink the water!"

"He's mad!"

*"Mama!!!"*

Vita put on the light in the pink room. She was very upset. In his nightmare, the boy had mistaken her for his mother. He must pay for that. She grabbed a pink robe from the pink closet and covered her nakedness. She towered like an Amazon warrior over the helpless Ganymede sprawled naked on the carpeted pink floor. The boy started to come to.

The boy did not look like a squatter, Vita observed. He looked more like a cherub in a Boticelli painting with his haunting gaze fixed on the ceiling. The pious woman remembered her fantasy of the two angels with the flaming swords keeping watch at the gate of Paradise east of Eden. She smiled wickedly and rummaged through the drawers. She bound the hands of the boy and, before he could react, she also tied his feet. She held his quivering body like a rag doll and pinned him against the pink wall.

"Lick my breast," she commanded, cupping her left breast close to his lips.

He did not move, thinking it was still part of his nightmare.

"Lick my navel."

He looked at her navel with disgust.

Vita eyed his limp member with contempt.

"*Vamos a ver,*" she snarled. She tied pink ribbons around his bound hands and his bound feet. She followed this move by stuffing his mouth with a pink Berthold Almagro T-shirt.

"God," Ganymede muttered, "let me wake up." As a nightmare, it was too heavy for his inexperienced mind. The woman was standing before him, holding a whip in her right hand and a humongous plastic phallus in her left, which appeared to Ganymede like a snake ready to leap and strike him.

"If you will cooperate," she said, "I'll not use the whip. If you won't, you'll be salvaged as a Hugo loyalist squatter plotting to assassinate President Girlie."

The woman rolled the wriggling, bound and gagged boy over so that he ended up lying on his stomach. Triumphant, she switched on the dildo. The gadget forced itself into Ganymede's sphincter and his mind spun with a mixture of horror and excitement.

"God, this is real," Ganymede whimpered.

The boy struggled very hard and tensed his buttocks to expel the gadget, but it only went deeper.

Ganymede saw on the wall the picture of Madame Girlie

Chichi Vda. de Almagro and his body ached with inexorable pain.

*"Mama!"* he cried.

Enraged, Vita kicked the thighs of the boy twice and slapped his face thrice. For emptying his bladder on her pink carpet, she whipped him several times until she got tired.

Two blocks away from Second Coming, a cigarette vendor was glued to her transistor radio. She was intently hanging on to every word of President Hugo whose tape-recorded message to his followers was being played in one of the two stations that welcomed loyalist block timers. It was timed to air during the loyalist march for the return of President Hugo.

The vendor shed a tear. Her husband had been dismissed from his job at city hall; she herself lost hers as a Metro Aide sweeping the streets of the capital. The revolutionary government had evicted them from the piece of land that President Hugo had granted them through a land for the landless initiative of the First Lady. She had heard that the officer-in-charge of the Metropolitan Commission would soon run after sidewalk vendors like her.

"God," the woman vendor prayed, "please bring back President Hugo. Bring back our real president."

President Hugo's ouster by no means did not come about in a vacuum, she admitted to herself. He started his first term with so much promise, building much-needed infrastructures. He dreamed of bringing Islas e Islotes into the club of newly industrializing countries. But whatever progress was made was soon overtaken by the burden of servicing the crushing foreign debts that he had incurred trying to pursue his vision to make this country great again.

He extended his rule by declaring martial law while the country's economy languished, driving millions of his countrymen to look for work in all corners of the world. He battled a communist and a Muslim rebellion while his close associates helped themselves to the nation's coffers.

President Hugo's grave miscalculation was in believing that he alone could solve the country's problems, and he overstayed his welcome by staying in power for twenty long years.

But the revolutionary government did not love the poor. The foreign observers were duped into believing that the poor had voted for President Hugo because he had bought their votes.

The woman felt orphaned. This never happened before. In the old days they could afford to eat three square meals a day. Now, they were lucky if they could eat one meal of their daily subsistence of rice and dried fish. How could they survive? Their children had resorted to begging. They lived under a bridge. Her husband had been missing for a week. The freedom march grew louder.

# CHAPTER VI

# The Highest Form of Chivalry

ATHER MORÁN'S ALARM CLOCK ON HIS bedside table was set to ring at five thirty in the morning. At four o'clock, the friar, dressed in his religious habit, was already praying the breviary. As he prayed, he slowly paced back and forth inside his room, his lips moving audibly. He could relate to every word of the breviary.

The friars had the obligation to pray the Lauds, their morning prayer, and the Matins, their night prayer, in common. Praying the breviary was a community act that demanded the presence of every member of the community. To lessen the burden of their daily parish work, the friars had done away with the daytime prayer, provided each friar said it on his own.

During the snap elections, Father Tiburron dropped the Lauds and the Matins from the regular schedule without the approval of the community. Because money talked louder than God, whose silence allows sinners to damn themselves, God was relegated to the sacristy for the deification of pink goddess Madame Girlie Chichi Vda. de Almagro, anointed by Archbishop Khoneimo to be the redeemer of all her fellow inhabitants of the benighted Islas e Islotes. The Archbishop had assured the people that the pink messiah would deliver Islas e Islotes from poverty, disease, famine, pestilence, plague, drought, earthquake, fire, insurgency, *tsunami*, graft and corruption, pornography, foreign debt and other natural and man-made calamities bequeathed them by the Hugos and their cronies.

The foreign correspondents sang hosanna to Madame Girlie Chichi Vda. de Almagro, enamored as they were with the idea of pitting a widow against what they considered a formidable strongman. Those who had extrapolated the election returns to suit the Archbishop's *vox populi vox Dei* show of force were amply rewarded with enviable positions in the government.

⁂

The temporal crusade of Archbishop Khoneimo to establish an earthly kingdom here on earth was realized when President Hugo was delivered by his own trusted lieutenants, Defense Minister Pablo Comdolezzo and Lieutenant General Fidelito Bilario, to the most powerful nation on earth notorious for its bullying tactics against smaller nations like Islas e Islotes.

Before the campaign for the snap elections, Minister Comdolezzo expected himself to be picked as Hugo's vice presidential running mate. But Hugo instead chose Art Chavezcu, an octogenarian and well-respected constitutional expert. Stung by what he considered as a ringing rejection by the president, he consulted his former mentor, Rafaelito Salazar, who was now holding a high position as director of the World Council's commission on population in New York.

Salazar told Comdolezzo: "My friend, follow your conscience."

He gave this piece of advice when it became clear to him that his former acolyte had become bitter for being ignored by President Hugo in favor of an elderly politician not for any reason other than to please the Gringolanders who viewed Comdolezzo unacceptable. To them, he was a human rights violator on account of his former role as martial law administrator. Not even his law degree from Harvard could improve his standing before the eyes of the Gringolanders who were careful not to be seen as glossing over human rights violations in favor of a quick victory against the communist rebels.

After Salazar had resigned his post as chief of staff of President Hugo, a number of international organizations had a bidding war to get him on board. He opted to head the newly created population commission where he developed a controversial program to distribute condoms and other forms of contraception in Third World countries. Despite opposition from the Church and pro-life groups, it proved so successful according to the metrics set by the World Council itself that people back home began thinking of him as a serious presidential contender should he decide to run.

Salazar had resigned from the Hugo Cabinet seventeen years earlier instead of yielding to intense pressure from some Red Ladies and their powerful husbands who formed the president's inner circle to get himself involved in a fertilizer scam. As head of a Cabinet sub-committee tasked to achieve self-sufficiency in rice production within three years, he accomplished it in an incredibly short span of less than twenty-four months. By any stretch of the imagination, he was no Superman; he simply implemented the blueprint that had been in place for years but was mired in red tape. With a generous aid from the Earth Bank, rice farmers were given affordable loans at near zero interest rates to buy tractors, mechanized rice harvesters and threshers and other farm machinery. Expert advice was at their disposal at taxpayers' expense.

His achievement made him a darling of the press, who gave him "the food czar" moniker, which made the agriculture minister resentful and very angry because he wanted the glory for himself so that he could easily and unquestionably inflate the fertilizer subsidies given to farmers and pocket most of it for himself and other corrupt ministers.

Shortly after President Hugo was ousted from power, Salazar left New York to visit the capital of Gringolandia to discuss with close advisers and with Gringolander admirers his next move. For growing louder was the clamor for him to come home to play a significant political role — even run for president in the next elections — in the post-Hugo government of Madame Girlie Chichi Vda. de Almagro. But on the eve of his departure to Islas e Islotes, he dropped dead in his hotel room. He died of cardiac arrest. His sudden death left Comdolezzo even more bitter and depressed, for now he felt completely lost without his sage, lifelong mentor.

Rather foolishly, he would later join various military attempts to topple Madame Girlie Chichi Vda. de Almagro from power but none of these attempts ever succeeded because the military leaders behind them fought with their mouths rather than their guns. They paid dearly for their indiscretion because it enabled the Pink Tiger and the regular Army to read their game plan. On their seventh, bloodiest and near-successful attempt to topple the Girlie government, the coup plotters would lose their godfather in the Cabinet.

Madame Girlie Chichi Vda. de Almagro fired Minister Comdolezzo after summoning him to the palace while government forces were conducting mopping up operations against the remnants of the failed putsch. She replaced him with General Bilario, who threw Comdolezzo under the bus to be the "protector and defender of President Girlie." The defense portfolio moved him closer to his desire to be president.

Snatching her gasping government from the claws of defeat, Gringolandia flew four unmarked F-16 fighter jets over the capital to provide air cover to government forces that proceeded to rout the rebel soldiers. Rebel defeat at the mere appearance of the four F-16 fighter jets that did not even fire a single missile gave Madame Girlie Chichi Vda. de Almagro the courage to give Comdolezzo the boot, who could do nothing but to submit himself to his fate.

After the "Girlie Miracle," it had become the eleventh commandment, engraved in the hearts of the pink chosen people, to venerate Madame Girlie Chichi Vda. de Almagro because, as what Archbishop Khoneimo claimed, she was a living saint.

Servants of the Lord who had forged an unholy alliance with the rebels to destroy the Hugos spouted venom from their pulpits and condemned the exiled president and the First Lady including all those identified with them, from their friends, business cronies, allies and supporters, not excluding the lowliest squatters who voted Hugo-Chavezcu during the snap elections.

***

To play on the inherent religiosity of the islanders, Archbishop Khoneimo portrayed Madame Girlie Chichi Vda. de Almagro as the amalgam of Joan of Arc and the mother of Jesus Christ who did not need to undergo a crucifixion because she herself smashed the serpent by crucifying Hugo the devil incarnate to the last nail. In the euphoria that followed the "Girlie Miracle," the first commandment given by God the Father to Moses on Mount Sinai, *I am the Lord your God, you shall not have strange gods before me,* became for the Girlie worshippers as acrimonious as the Council of Trent.

Having finished with the Lauds, Father Morán pulled a chair and sat down before his working table. What am I doing with my life?

The friar tinkered with the keyboard of his laptop, an ordination gift from Father Mark, the editor of a magazine for which he wrote a monthly column. It was Father Mark who vouched for Ganymede's entrance to the minor seminary of his religious congregation. The laptop had been his sole material possession since he joined the religious life. Father Morán had always been happy with his priesthood of literature, but now he realized that he had not written any single line ever since the Girlie takeover. He could not write in an atmosphere of hatred and deceit, where everything unreal was passed off as real. The institutional Church in Islas e Islotes had become an agent of the *de facto* regime. Its religious leaders had wittingly or unwittingly encouraged the worship of false gods by rendering to Caesar what belonged to God and to God what belonged to Caesar. This was not Father Morán's idea of the holy priesthood. This was not his concept of religion. He found himself rebelling against the pharisaical system that some religious leaders, encouraged by the Girlie regime, were determined to establish.

The friar started typing something on a letter-size bond paper. Anything. "The quick brown fox jumps over the lazy dog near the bank of the river." No, in this atmosphere he could not write a single poem. He felt terribly alone and lonely.

⁂

As a junior high school student he was a walking success. Aside from being class president, he was the celebrated campus poet. His poems captivated the hearts of girls. Nothing was required of him to set the heart of girls a-flutter. All he needed to do was to write for them a poem. His love poem was sure to conquer any girl's heart.

"Who do you admire?"

"I admire a girl who can sing like a nightingale, is as fair as cherry blossoms, as silent as beautiful dawn."

The interview on the girl he admired got published on the front page of their student paper, prominently boxed.

The friends of Azucena told her she was the girl he admired. Aside from being the top student of the sophomore class, she was the best singer in school.

The friends of Cherry told her she was the girl he admired. She was his cherry blossoms, and she was very fair.

The friends of Bella Aurora told her she was the girl he admired. Her name was Spanish for "beautiful dawn."

"You're getting nowhere in your studies!" his father thundered.

His father wanted him to be a scholar, just like his elder brother.

"My lowest grade is ninety-one."

"Your brother's lowest grade during this grading period is

ninety-five. Don't deceive yourself. Stop writing poems. You can't live on your love poems. I want you to be a certified public accountant."

"I don't want figures."

"You can't survive without them."

He seethed with rebellion. His father did not want any artist around. He did not like any of his children to follow in the footsteps of their maternal grandfather Eliodoro who spent his time painting sunsets and lovely maidens.

He started his senior year in high school by announcing that he was not going to run for the presidency of the supreme student council. He stopped writing love poems. Instead, he wrote prose-poems dedicated to the Blessed Virgin Mary.

All his teachers were Bible Baptists.

His prose-poems alarmed his teachers. He was called to the faculty room by their class adviser, a Bible-thumping zealot. He wanted to blame the loss of his grandparents' fortune on his becoming a Roman Catholic. The adviser did all the talking and was not interested in hearing his side. "I thought you would be another Byron," he said, "but I'm disappointed. What's this I hear that you're going to be a priest? Too bad you're not my grandchild. Otherwise, I could have sent you to jail. Your popish friends have ruined your future. Repent and be converted! Separate from those anti-Christ. That's the most logical way to get back your fortune. God will reward you abundantly."

He became an outcast. His rivals for the honor roll jeered at him. The parents of Azucena, Cherry and Bella Aurora forbade their daughters from going out with him. "The Pope," the history teacher told their class, "is the anti-Christ of the Bible. The harlot is the Roman Catholic Church."

No matter how hard he studied, he could not land on top of the honor roll, even if he topped the division tests. The teachers always had reasons: his character, his attitude in life, his stubbornness. He did not march to receive his diploma. His grade in character education was barely passing. He was ostracized along with the flunkers who had taken him as their comrade. They asked him to ghostwrite love letters to their seemingly unreachable crushes.

Enrolled as a freshman in a university far from home, he frequented the cafeteria where one day, while sipping orange juice, he looked up and noticed a good-looking girl seated across from him at the table. They said "hi" to each other and that initial encounter led to more meetings that developed into a friendship. Her face exuded the loveliness of life. She was the managing editor of the university publication.

Her name was Elinore. She rarely talked to others, but she kidded around a lot when they were together. She was a campus figure, a scholar and the most exalted sister of the Sigma Phi Sorority. She recruited him to join the Sigma Chi, a brother fraternity. They enjoyed each other's company.

"I like your eyes, brod," she said. "They're the eyes of a sensitive soul."

Elinore was a poet and wrote much better poetry than Ernie Virtuoso, the know-it-all editor of the school paper who never hesitated to put the less knowledgeable on the spot.

"I like your poems."

"Life's a bubble," she said. "The best things in life are free, but you've to fight for them every day. We're as good as today. Brod, here's a novena to Saint Therese of the Child Jesus. Make a wish."

He did not make a wish. Instead, he mentally made a deal with the saint that if he received three red roses after three days, he would take it as a sign that God wanted him to become a priest. Three days later at class, their professor, a priest, was late. While the class was waiting for him, a beautiful young woman with three red roses walked into the classroom and asked for one José Morán. He presented himself to the young woman, who handed him the three red roses and an envelope. It contained a love poem dedicated to him and simply signed, "Elinore."

"What are you reading?" the professor asked as he snatched the poem from his hand. The priest had arrived fifteen minutes late and was in a bad mood. He held on to the roses until he got pricked by their thorns. Then José Morán remembered his deal with Saint Therese.

"You're in love with the idea that you're in love," Father Felipe Triste, the university publications moderator, said as he closed the door behind them. "You're only a brat," the priest sat down and faced him in a very condescending manner. "Stop seeing Elinore. I've better plans for her. I want her to be the next editor. Don't destroy her future."

It was raining very hard and how he desperately wanted to bolt from the office, to run away from it all, to evaporate, but the rain fell harder. The baby typhoon had gathered strength.

"How old are you, *child*?" the priest inquired as though wanting to make him feel guilty about his age. "Stop harboring any idea that you'll be another Shakespeare."

"I'll stop bothering her," he assured the priest. He did not want any trouble, so he tried avoiding her. But she kept pursuing him, sending him more love poems and more red roses, always coming in three's.

"I'm going to become a priest."

"Are you crazy?"

When he told her about his deal with Saint Therese, she cried in disbelief. Between sobs she said, "Brod, don't be superstitious."

She snatched from him the copy of the novena she had given him so she could tear it to pieces. A piece of paper tucked in the novena came out flying. Out of curiosity, she silently read what was scribbled there. Her eyes opened wide when she read what turned out to be a draft.

"Years ago, I yearned to be inside those walls, to don the garment of the wise, who search their end in him. I want to be among his shepherds, tender of the invaluable flock, and in the evening to clutch the stars, to put again the world into correction."

"That's poetry!" she exclaimed. She allowed him to kiss her on the lips. They kissed long.

"Brod," she said jestingly, "you think you can still write poems there? You think you can make your life a priesthood of literature?" He kissed her again to stop her from asking more questions.

The pedantic editor suspected something was going on between the two and conferred with the father moderator. Both of them were grooming Elinore to be the next editor and feared that her palling around with José Morán would distract her from that goal and ruin her chances of clinching the competitive post.

"He has grown cocky," the editor said. "He thinks he's Robert Browning."

"He feels obviously flattered," the moderator said.

The priest altogether stopped talking to him. He let the editor post a warning sign, handwritten in black marker, above the blackboard that said: **IT IS STRICTLY FORBIDDEN TO FALL IN LOVE IN THIS OFFICE.**

It was sunset when they last parted. Elinore never thought she would ever see him again. She was in her usual bubbly mood, although it was obvious that she did not want to show what she really felt.

He felt the urge to look back, to tell her he could still serve God by loving his fellowmen. But his will prevailed over his heart. Something in him seemed missing, but he kept on walking ahead. There was no turning back.

⁓✍⁓

There she was, his grandmother Francisca, groping for his face, his eyes, his nose, his mouth, his ears, his forehead. She had memorized his features the day he was born. She had lost her sight, so she wanted to be sure he was indeed her favorite grandson.

His grandmother Francisca! Sweet as the earth after the rain, her presence would bloom from dawn to dusk. For playmates she gave him Snow White and the Seven Dwarfs, Pinocchio, too, to learn his ABCs. Rewinding the kingdom of Ante-Porticum, she taught him the gallantry of knights. He must not laugh at Cinderella breaking plates. He must awaken Sleeping Beauty with a kiss.

His grandmother Francisca! She was the garden his grand-father loved to paint. He was her Little Boy Blue pursued by Furies but enamored to seek the highest form of chivalry.

"It's you, my dearest boy," she said, "It's you, all right."

He wanted to cry, but he did not want to make her sad. She had always told him when he was still a kid that men do not cry. "You must be brave," she told him one soccer game. "Life is more than playing 'It.'" He made her laugh, instead, by telling her jokes he had heard from fellow aspirants.

"You've not changed," she said. "You're still my dearest child." She loved him more than all her children and grand-children combined.

"Should I become a priest?" he asked her. "Do you want me to be a priest? I can stay here and give you company. I can leave the seminary."

When he entered the seminary, his Uncle Ernesto died in their coffee plantation, hacked to death by two bolo men. Two other deaths in the family followed in quick succession: Kakak, their deaf-mute adopted sister, and his grandfather Eliodoro passed away. He was not with them in their final moments. He wanted badly to be with his grandmother when the time came. He knew she did not have much time left.

"Be a priest. A priest with a mission!"

"You're a Bible Baptist."

"The word of God has no religion. We're all children of God."

She held his hand.

"Once you're a priest, never abandon the exiled, the desti-tute, the oppressed." She spoke from her own experience. She had lost all her properties. She is one of them.

He kissed her hand.

"Would you want to be baptized Catholic?"

"If you want me to."

"Faith's something personal. What's your personal decision?"

"No." She was as firm as a rock.

"Why?"

"Catholics always pray to saints, they forget to pray to God. They pray *'Ave Maria purísima, sin pecado concebida,'* but they're damned because of their idolatry."

She laughed at what she had uttered. Her laughter was infectious. He laughed with her.

"But why have you never opposed my decision to become a priest?"

"Because I know God has a mission for you. Cleanse the Roman Catholic Church. Bring to the Catholics the One True God. Use your pen. Write the truth. Spread love. To spread the Gospel of love is the highest form of chivalry."

His grandmother Francisca! He was so proud of her. She spoke Spanish and learned English from the first American Christian missionaries who came to Islas e Islotes at the start of the last century.

"Are you sure you'll be saved as a Bible Baptist?"

"Oh, the hope of life eternal," she started singing. "In the land beyond our sight. Living streams and pastures vernal, songs and visions of delight. In the home of many mansions, in the halls of love and light."

The onslaughts of the years had not changed her voice. She could still sing like a nightingale. She was still as fair as cherry blossoms. She had something of an ethereal glow about her.

"Are you sure…"

"As sure as the sun rises, I'll be saved."

"But I've got to be at least ninety-nine point ninety-nine percent sure that you'll be saved."

"Read Romans 6:21-23."

He opened his *New American Bible* and read: "When you were slaves of sin, you had freedom from justice. What benefit did you then enjoy? Things you are now ashamed of, all of them tending toward death. But now that you are freed from sin and have become slaves of God, you tend toward eternal life. The wages of sin is death, but the gift of God is eternal life in Christ Jesus our Lord."

"Not from the King James version," she said, "but anyway the word of God is beautiful in all versions of the Bible. I've complete trust in the Lord that he'll save me, I've never wished ill of anyone. I've given my goods to the poor. I've loved much. I'm sure one hundred percent that I'll be saved as a Bible Baptist."

"Then remain a Bible Baptist. You might not go to heaven if you would turn Roman Catholic."

"I know you'll make a holy priest. Read Philippians 3:20."

"As you well know, we have our citizenship in heaven; it is from there that we eagerly await the coming of our Saviour, the Lord Jesus Christ."

"Wherever your mission is, don't forget that although you're born here in Islas e Islotes, you're also a citizen of the world and would eventually become a citizen of heaven."

She did not even give him the chance to cry. She died the moment he was accepted to the novitiate. Since novices were not allowed to stay out of the novitiate house for more than twenty-four hours, he could not go to the province for her funeral.

What am I doing with my life? He mused. The clock sounded the alarm. He opened the door and stepped out of his room. The Mass would start at six.

# CHAPTER VII

# Pink Magnificat

SISTER PIEDAD WENT TO HEAR MASS that afternoon to pray for Hugo loyalist freedom marchers who were on their way to Mount Banaag. She had received a vision that death would befall many a loyalist once they passed Hacienda Candelabra, the stronghold of the Almagros. Sister Piedad once reigned as Muse of the Night during their town fiesta. An heiress of one of the privileged families of Dinagyang province, she once had the vocation to be a nun while still a fifteen-year-old student in an exclusive school. She postponed her decision to enter the nunnery until after her debut, when she would seek the permission of her parents to allow her to join the convent as their birthday gift to her.

Piedad's debut was celebrated with all the pageantry worthy of a beauty queen. On her way to blow the candles and cut the birthday cake, she tripped on the carpet. A young Army sergeant helped her up. He escorted her to the table where the birthday cake with eighteen candles was waiting to be cut into eighteen slices to be distributed by eighteen little girls dressed as angels to eighteen winners of that night's birthday raffles.

Piedad and the sergeant knew from the very start that it was love at first sight. After dancing with the serviceman, the debutante thanked God for the Lord's birthday gift to her: Sergeant Donato Manes. Right there and then the sergeant proposed marriage. The young woman told him to wait until she turned twenty-one.

On Piedad's twenty-first birthday, she got married to Donato.

Knowing about his wife's dream to become a nun, Donato suggested that they offer to the Lord their first-born, a baby boy whom they named Pelagio.

Pelagio, it was said, could foretell what would come to pass. He told his parents, while he was still in grade school, that he wanted to become a priest.

He said his father would become a colonel and die fighting the communists.

The church was standing-room only when Sister Piedad arrived. She knelt on the last pew and prayed fervently for the safety of all the freedom marchers. Her son Pelagio had joined them. Ganymede Morán stood by the church door together with Lieutenant Evans Marfori, a loyalist sympathizer.

Vita Marcelo did not have Ganymede killed. After beating the boy up for peeing on the pink carpet in the pink room, she dragged him by the hair to the bathroom and gave him golden showers. Not knowing what to do with him next, she shaved his head and got rid of his man-hair. She bathed the boy clean and powdered him from head to foot. She then called for three members of the salvage team of the Pink Tiger who alternated as live sex performers and bouncers and instructed them never

to touch a hair of the boy and laughed with the men upon realizing that she had left no hair on his body for them to touch.
She told them to drop the boy just as he was, in his birthday
suit, at the back of the Cultural Center.

Lieutenant Marfori was on his regular morning jog when
he chanced upon a shivering Ganymede. When he learned that
he was a loyalist, he invited the disoriented youth to his bach-
elor's pad in Tres Gatos to regain his strength. But first he took
him to an Army clinic that treated Ganymede's slight injuries
at the hands of Vita and of her henchmen. He learned that
the young man's father and siblings were joining the freedom
march and that his mother was left home alone. He did not
want Ganymede to return home in his condition as it would
worry his mother.

That afternoon, after looking in vain for Tess Segismundo
— the address she had given him turned out to be the resi-
dence of Roy Gernale, founder of Hugo Forever that provided
security to loyalist rallies — Lieutenant Marfori was not easily
discouraged. He and Ganymede had been to Roy's house at
Hinugyaw. Nobody was there except the maid who had never
heard of a Tess Segismundo. The whole Gernale family had
joined the freedom marchers.

On their way back to Lieutenant Marfori's apartment, he and
Ganymede decided to drop by a church to pray, the same
house of worship where Georgina and Jessie had agreed to
meet because that was the most convenient place for Rudolph
Rivera who was set to interview them on the Hugo loyalist
phenomenon.

Georgina and Jessie had gathered several boxes of medicine, canned foods, slippers and soap bars for the freedom marchers. Together with the journalist, they would meet the marchers at Hacienda Candelabra.

Rudolph's military sources had tipped him off about classified intelligence reports that the Pink Tiger would provoke Hugo loyalists into violence once they reached Hacienda Candelabra.

Georgina and Jessie were undaunted. No force on earth could prevent them from giving aid to the Hugo loyalists when they needed it most. They knelt on the last pew near the church door. They had to wait for Rudolph.

The church was like a marketplace. Wearing pink headbands, characters from exclusive schools acted as if they owned the place. The papal flag was displayed side by side with the flag of the republic, strung with pink ribbons, at the tabernacle.

Ten catechists in pink dresses lined up on the aisles, each carrying a collection plate. Donations from abroad, in cash or in kind, had reached an equivalent of fifty million pesos, but Archbishop Khoneimo wanted to squeeze fifty million pesos more from the one hundred twenty million inhabitants of Islas e Islotes over whom he laid claim to be the undisputed "spiritual leader."

Prim and proper in her school uniform but looking stoned, Megan Reynoso emerged from the sacristy to distribute copies of the "Pink Magnificat." She was escorted by four long-haired, post-pubescent boys her age. Like her, they also looked high on drugs. The chandeliers were lighted. Trance music wafted in the air. Flashing the pink sign — a raised right hand with the thumb and index finger sticking out to form an uneven V-sign and with the remaining three fingers clenched on the palm — Sister Bruhilda sashayed from the presbytery and whipped up the pink crowd into cheering: *"Gir-lie! Gir-lie! Gir-lie! Gir-lie!"*

She was at once a goddess of war beating the war drums to terrify the vanquished. Mothers with their babies who had gone to the church to pray took off with their little ones without once looking back. Their infants cried in chorus, terrified by the appearance of Sister Bruhilda and the unearthly noise she and her pink congregation were generating.

"Let's now pray the 'Pink Magnificat,'" Sister Bruhilda warmed the congregation up. "Before we start with the pink Mass proper, let's rehearse this prayer. I'm the bride of Christ speaking, so you must follow me."

"Amen," the crowd responded without contesting the logic of the nun's command. "Our whole being proclaims the greatness of the Lord, our spirit overflows with joy in God, our Savior. For he has compassion on our country's misery, so now, we have regained our natural dignity. God who is mighty has done miracles for us, holy is his name. His mercy is from age to age on every nation that hopes in him. He has shown might with his arm; he has confused the cronies in their innermost thoughts. He has deposed the Hugos from their thrones and has restored our freedom and self-esteem. He has revealed to Gringolanders our great hidden power to achieve national reconciliation when we use non-violent weapons of united prayers and friendly dialogue, of courageous sacrifice and love of country, of mutual trust and respect, of sincere forgiveness and friendship. Therefore all nations shall call us maturing

Christians and glorify you, Lord, God of history. Glory to the Father, and to the Son, and to the Holy Spirit. As it was in the beginning, is now, and will be forever. Amen."

Sister Piedad recognized Sister Bruhilda as the nun who had incited the pink thugs to terrorize the Hugo loyalists during the first of May rally. The nun also figured in the violent dispersal of the loyalists by the Pink Tiger.

For the pink government, it was perfectly all right to carry images of the Blessed Virgin Mary and to pray the rosary in their demonstrations against President Hugo, but a crime when done against the Girlie government. The pink thugs did not spare Sister Piedad's images of Jesus, Mary and Joseph. Sister Bruhilda had ordered the pink crowd to burn the religious images because, she said, they belonged to the devil.

Truth was, the images had been blessed by Cardinal Rufus, the first prince of the Church from Islas e Islotes, the day before he died.

From the sacristy Vita Marcelo took her seat of honor as reader. Sister Bruhilda served as commentator. The Tiples of Father Nico sang "Onward, Christian Soldiers" with the pitch of the *castrati* back in the days when young boys were subjected to the barbarity of castration before puberty in order to turn them into boy sopranos.

Twelve altar boys came out of the sacristy, followed by Father Nico vested in pink chasuble and pink stole exclusively fashioned for him by the best of the best couturiers in Islas e Islotes.

Father Nico genuflected before the tabernacle, kissed the altar and adjusted the microphone. "Ladies and gentlemen," he began in modulated voice, "this Mass is for sinless people only. The Hugo loyalists, if they ever made the mistake of being around, are requested to leave the church. This Mass is not for them."

There was a reason Father Nico took pains to modulate his voice. Like Father Tiburron who was missing an index finger, the source of his insecurity, Father Nico not only had a lisp but he also stuttered.

His classmates in theology had told the junior seminarians that his impediment was caused by a very short tongue, and whenever they had public disagreements with him, often triggered by his macho brand of rough and tumble basketball where his elbows were always landing on the chins of the opposing team, they would scream at him at the top of their lungs: *"Stutterer!!! Lisping snake!!!"*

It was their cruel way of getting even with him, and it was enough for the then Brother Rembert to turn tail and to profusely apologize. The younger seminarians always looked away and pretended not to hear. They knew he was up for promotion as a Father Master and did not want to be on his bad side. Besides modulating his voice to sound as macho as he could, he also made it a point to be the first one to ridicule any seminarian who appeared effeminate.

He was quick with a ready put-down to call attention to what he considered the feminine ways of those he had taken delight in making fun of.

"Stop walking life a faggot," he would say to someone while following him, always making sure impressionable high school freshmen were within hearing distance to provide an approving chorus of laughter for dramatic effect.

"Man up!" he would yell to another, who had just missed a free throw in a basketball game.

Rudolph arrived and immediately spotted Georgina and Jessie near the confessional.

"In the name of the Father, and of the Son, and of the Holy Spirit," Father Nico read from the missal, this time in his naturally high-pitched voice that prevailed over his initial attempt at modulation.

"Amen," responded the altar boys.

"My brothers and sisters, let's offer this Mass for the heroes of the Girlie Revolution, namely, us. We've put the dictator and his profligate wife to flight. Let's congratulate ourselves for being among the living heroes of our history, for being among the living saints. The....the...Lord be...be...with you."

The priest got so distracted by the giggly altar boys that he began to lisp and to stutter.

"And with your spirit."

The Tiples of Father Nico sang the "Kyrie" and the "Gloria." Lieutenant Marfori foresaw that the Mass was going to be unpredictable and longer than the usual Masses he was used to hear.

He tapped Ganymede on the shoulder, a signal that they must leave pronto.

Ganymede was in disbelief as he was listening to Father Nico spout his venom from the pulpit.

This was the same Father Nico in the middle of an unprecedented sex scandal in a seminary known for its holy religious priests and brothers who used the computer and other means of social communications in their work of evangelization.

Unbeknown to Father Nico, the Assistant Prefect of Studies and the professed students who had saved him from the hands of the Firenze brothers were the very first ones to inform everybody and their uncle about what had happened. Putting on the maudlin and solemn face that religious hypocrites like them would normally reserve to be worn only on Good Friday, Father Nico's brother religious had assured him that his secret was safe with them and should not go any farther than the Father Provincial and Council.

But as soon as they had taken him to the quarters of the nuns who applied first aid to his injuries, they started texting everyone they knew, including Ganymede, about the sex abuse incident.

When memory of the scandal almost faded with time years later, Father Nico would take to Virtual Book of Faces and troll the social media site searching for his former seminarians. He learned that they had created an alumni page on the popular site. He pretended to be concerned with their spiritual well-being, asking them how life was treating them or some such inane questions.

Knowing the propensity of many current and former seminarians for gossip — for what is there left to do in the seminary besides the repetitive tasks of school work, reading, prayer and meditation, some limited TV and sports and recreation? — Father Morán could imagine the former seminarians snickering whenever Father Nico tried his old trick. But in his self-absorption, Father Nico never fully understood why no one wanted to have anything to do with him.

Psychologists say that self-centeredness, such as that possessed in excess by Father Nico, is a common characteristic among pedophiles, and it enables them to excuse their behavior and to project blame onto their victims with total lack of empathy.

⸎

From where she was perched like a Gorgon looking for her next victim, Vita recognized the boy she had humbled inside the pink room. She followed him with her gaze when she saw him leave with the older, muscular man whose posture reminded her of a presidential *aide-de-camp* that she fancied in the palace. She stripped them naked in her thoughts, and imagined them to be the two angels east of Eden simultaneously impaling her every pore with their flaming swords. The heat she felt in her loins made her giddy and feverish.

Ganymede at first failed to recognize Vita, but once he sighted her, obscene images crossed his young mind. And the nun who called herself "bride of Christ" looked real scary. Father Rembert! Did he also examine with his magnifying glass those twelve giggly, girlish altar boys? Everything seemed absurd and surreal. Was the world going to an end?

He shook with terror. Lieutenant Marfori had to calm him down to prevent him from running from it all and being hit by the passing vehicles.

Vita did the first reading. It was from Exodus. The responsorial psalm was from Exodus. The Gospel was from Exodus. After the abduction of the Hugos into a life of exile, the Archbishop during his televised thanksgiving Mass substituted the Gospel reading with passages from Exodus. Priests like Father Nico who revered him followed his example. The decision to tinker with the liturgy was in line with the plan of then candidate Girlie's handlers to cast the campaign as a fight between Good and Evil. They wanted to portray President Hugo as the biblical pharaoh being confronted by candidate Girlie, the modern-day female Moses, as in the book of Exodus.

"Then the Lord said unto Moses, Go in unto Pharaoh, and tell him, Thus saith the Lord God of the Hebrews, Let my people go, that they may serve me."

Father Nico's homily left a bad taste in Rudolph's mouth with its icky mudslinging.

"My dear brothers and sisters in Jesus: The Hugo loyalists are spreading rumors that I'm a playboy, that I've plenty of children from different women. For this reason, I've adopted a male teenager to protect me from unreasonable women. He's now living with my parents as part of the family. These Hugo loyalists are at it again — spreading rumors. Don't believe them. They're only less than human. They refuse to think. They spread rumors without verification of facts. They anticipate without investigating. Don't they know that by criticizing a priest like me they're also criticizing God? Without us priests they can never go to heaven. Heaven is shut to sinners like them. Our country suffers because of these Hugo loyalists. They join rallies because they're being paid. Hugo forever? *Say what???* *Ha! Ha! Ha!*"

Sister Bruhilda led the congregation in flashing the signature Girlie sign and in shouting *"Gir-lie! Gir-lie! Gir-lie! Gir-lie!"*

*"Down with Hugo! Down with Hugo! Down with Hugo! Down with Hugo!"* Father Nico shrieked, flashing the pink sign in abandon, forgetting that President Hugo had already been forced into exile, abducted by his rescuers and plunked on the island paradise of Nuncamuere.

The Tiples of Father Nico burst into "Onward, Christian Soldiers" and drowned the voice of the congregation. After the pink faithful had quieted down, Father Nico went ahead with his homily.

"The Hugos should be made accountable for every conceivable evil that has befallen our impoverished nation. They squandered our patrimony and plundered our natural resources. Everyone here present, including me, of course, is suffering because of those thieves. The Hugos are thieves. *Thieves! Thieves! Thieves! Thieves!* They've no reason to live. They should disappear from the face of the earth."

*"Gir-lie! Gir-lie! Gir-lie! Gir-lie!"*

Vita was transported to another time when she was just a hanger-on in the palace. One day, while she was tearfully telling the First Lady about the blackmail threat from one of her lovers, a phone call on the First Lady's direct line interrupted their conversation. The exchange that followed remained embedded in her mind.

⚶

"Who is this?"

"The First Lady."
"Oh?"
"Could I do anything for you?"
"Are you really the First Lady?"
"Yes."
"No kidding?"
"This is the First Lady. Anything I can do for you?"
"If you're the First Lady, could you have the street in front of our boarding house fixed?"

"I'll hand over the phone to my social secretary. Tell her your complete name and your exact location so we can have the street fixed immediately."

It was a hyperactive boy on the other line with plenty of time on his hands who randomly dialed the number for fun. But his prank led to something good for his neighborhood. No less than the deputy governor of the metropolis, Julio Zetineb, was dispatched to see to it that the work was done.

"I'm sure," the boy bragged to his playmates, "it was the First Lady I just talked with."

Vita started sobbing.

"Yes, sister," Sister Bruhilda whispered to her. "Cry for the Hugos. There's no place for them here on earth. There'll be no place for them in heaven, either."

Vita fainted and had to be revived.

"Slain by the Spirit," Vita told the priest. Father Nico was ecstatic. He considered himself a holy priest, so his Mass must be by all means holy.

Georgina could not hold herself anymore. She went straight to Father Nico and complained. "Why don't you talk about God, about the Gospel, about love? You're inside the church, inside the house of God."

"Are you a loyalist?"

"Why?"

"Because you talk like one."

Sister Bruhilda was struck with terror. Was she seeing visions? The girl uncannily resembled the exiled First Lady, and the nun thought the First Lady had bilocated. She could not look at her face for long, so she settled for her feet. What was the size of her shoes? How many pairs of shoes did she own? Did she also know how to sing?

Georgina tore up her xerox copy of the new "Magnificat" and blew the shreds onto the face of the priest. Jessie held her by the hand and escorted her out of the church.

"This is an ungodly generation," Father Nico lamented. "My flock, do good for evil and ignore their recalcitrance. Their souls are already burning in hell."

⁂

At the farthest end of the church, Sister Piedad was lost in a trance. She thought she was levitating. "I'm levitating!" she screamed. The Tiples of Father Nico sang Handel's *Messiah*.

Soon everybody was kneeling down, making the sign of the cross and looking at Sister Piedad with awe and reverence, glorifying God for performing such a miracle before their sight.

Sister Bruhilda cast her eyes on Sister Piedad. This was the woman she heard on the first of May baying like a mare before the statues of Jesus, Mary and Joseph for the return of the Hugos. When Sister Bruhilda urged the riot police to fire the tear gas at Sister Piedad, the nun prayed the rosary. When the firemen aimed their hoses at the statues, the woman threw loaves of bread at them. The vestments of the statues flapped in the wind, and the water hit and knocked Sister Bruhilda down. Her bruises had been healed, and yet the scars remained. Who the hell could give this woman the power to levitate but Satan himself?

Sister Piedad somersaulted and gracefully landed on her feet like a seasoned gymnast to a standing ovation. The Tiples of Father Nico again sang Handel's *Messiah*. Even Father Nico was mesmerized. A living saint, he thought. He had a living saint among his pink congregation.

Everybody began speaking in tongues, but the glossolalia was cut short by the rending cry of Megan Reynoso. It came so suddenly and so piercingly loud that it scared the pigeons out of the church belfry. Confusion followed as Megan trashed on the floor, naked and laughing hysterically, calling out the name of Father José Morán.

# CHAPTER VIII

# Cult

JESSIE TOOK THE EASIER ROUTE to Dagung-cogon through the modern south superhighway built under the administration of President Hugo. With him on the front seat of his red Range Rover SUV was Rudolph. Seated alone on the back seat was Georgina.

The three young adults were scheduled to meet with the Reverend Pelagio Manes for Rudolph's series on the Hugo loyalist phenomenon. They would be his guests for a couple of days in the village of Paga.

The Reverend Manes was with the original ragtag band of Hugo loyalists when they organized the freedom march. He was back in Paga to lead its residents in welcoming the freedom marchers at the Rotunda del Sol.

That morning, the papers headlined the condemnation of the Reverend Manes by Archbishop Khoneimo. The prelate denounced the Reverend Manes and his cult "of fake priests and nuns." The Archbishop warned the public that the Reverend Manes was an instrument of Satan. His cult, the Archbishop said, was being funded by Hugo stragglers out to overthrow the Girlie government.

Gloria Singsonso had earlier wanted to go. Her sister Amparo, who was crowned the world's most beautiful woman a few years back, persuaded her to change her mind. Amparo was apolitical, but their mother was a turncoat. She used to hobnob with the First Lady and her Red Ladies, but when the Hugos got plopped in Nuncamuere she changed her standard color from red to pink. She likewise donated a beach house to Father Nico. When it became apparent that Gloria was getting more and more involved in working for the return of the Hugos, she was so disappointed with her favorite daughter she suffered a mild stroke. That was why Amparo was able to persuade her sister not to go to Paga.

"I won't turn on the car stereo" Jessie said. "Georgina can sing for us."

"Yes, Georgina," Rudolph said, "please sing for us 'As Time Goes By.'"

"No," Jessie said, "sing 'Sentimental Journey.'"

Georgina sang "The Way We Were."

Those were the days of the Good, the True and the Beautiful. Rudolph was an editor at the office of the press secretary in the palace, part of a special writers group crafting presidential statements. He helped conceptualize the tourism campaign that revolved around the slogan "Islas e Islotes: Beautiful Islands, Beautiful People." He used to cover the activities of the First Lady. In the process, he gathered many anecdotes about her, mostly eyewitness accounts.

When the smoke cleared after the Second World War, Peligro was one of the most devastated places one could imagine. As a little girl, the First Lady was in love with life. She took everything in stride. She was always singing. One day, while she was climbing a guava tree, singing "God Bless Islas e Islotes," she was hit by a pebble on her nape and the pain made her stop.

The stone thrower was nowhere to be found so the girl resumed her singing. A tall Gringolander with a big cigar passed by.

"Little girl," his voice boomed, "were you the one singing?"

"Yes, sir. I was singing until you passed by."

"Sing it again, please." She sang the same song.

"You were telling the truth. You were indeed the singer. Here, take some chocolate bars."

The following day, the big man with the big cigar came back with another Gringolander. They were looking for the girl who could sing. Radcliffe, a friend of the First Lady's family since her childhood, was there. He brought the two Gringolanders to the Red Sea, so named because thousands had drowned there during the liberation of Islas e Islotes by the Gringolanders. They found the girl on the beach, playing with the sand and singing "God Bless Islas e Islotes" at the top of her voice. Her audience was her brother Curcumo.

"Little girl," the big Gringolander introduced his companion, "this is my friend. He's a composer. Could you sing for him your favorite song?"

The girl sang "God Bless Islas e Islotes." Before she could continue her song, the composer interrupted her: "No, my little friend, it's not 'God Bless Islas e Islotes'; it's 'God Bless

Gringolandia,' not 'Islas e Islotes.'" He gave three bars of chocolate to her and a bar to Curcumo.

"No, it's 'God Bless Islas e Islotes,'" she insisted. "We sing that in school. Our teachers taught us to sing 'God Bless Islas e Islotes.'"

"I should know. I composed that song myself. I want it to be sung exactly the way I composed it."

The girl returned the bars of chocolate to the composer.

"If God can bless Gringolandia," the girl said, "why not Islas e Islotes also?"

"Right," the big Gringolander agreed with the little girl. Turning to the composer he said, "I suggest that you compose a special song for her. Right now. I want her to sing it tomorrow before our soldiers."

The composer sat on the beach and composed a song in an hour. He gave the lyrics to the girl and taught her the tune. They sang it together.

"If you memorize this song tonight," the composer said, "you'll sing tomorrow."

After an hour, the girl had memorized the lyrics and mastered the tune.

The big Gringolander was pleased with his singing discovery. He gently patted her on the head and jestingly said, "Future historians will never acknowledge me as the talent scout of this wonderful child."

The following day, the girl sang before a huge crowd of soldiers and civilians. She had two hundred soldiers for her backup. That was her first concert. The man who introduced her to the composer was the liberator of Islas e Islotes.

"Who threw the pebble that hit her on the nape and why?" Rudolph asked Radcliffe, who was in Paga to monitor the march and lend his support. "I did it to attract her attention to the presence of the Great Liberator in the area."

⚜

The Reverend Manes read Psalm 137: "By the streams of Babylon we sat and wept when we remembered Zion. On the aspens of the land we hung up our harps. Though there our captors asked of us the lyrics of our songs, and our despoilers urged us to be joyous: 'Sing for us the songs of Zion!' How could we sing a song of the Lord in a forgotten land? If I forget you, Jerusalem, may my right hand be forgotten! May my tongue cleave to my palate if I remember you not, if I place not Jerusalem ahead of my joy. Remember, 0 Lord, against the children of Edom, the day of Jerusalem when they said, 'Raze it, raze it down to the foundations!' 0 daughter of Babylon, you destroyer, happy the man who shall repay you the evil you have done for us! Happy the man who shall smash your little ones against the rock!"

Rudolph studied the faces of the members of the Reverend Manes's cult. They were all unsmiling and stern. The menfolk were garbed in priestly white soutane while the womenfolk in a nun's habit. Jessie noted the absence of pews in the chapel. The tabernacle was made of bamboo and the altar of polished coconut shells. A helicopter hovered above the valley.

"Don't be afraid," the Reverend Manes assured his followers. "The pilot is one of our members. He has forewarned me about the suspicion of the Archbishop that we're being funded by some generals still loyal to President Hugo. The Pink Tiger had sent me a pink shirt with pink ribbon and a handwritten threat presumably signed in blood."

Cults, like witchcraft, Rudolph mused, thrive on people's misery and gullibility. The more the group is persecuted, the more they get cohesive and united and fanatical to the cause their leaders espouse.

"This is an occupation government," the Reverend Manes continued. "We fight for President Hugo because we fight for God. We'll never allow the communist comrades of the usurper to destroy our faith in God. We'll never allow evildoers to play with our lives and to take possession of our souls."

⸎

After the Bible service, Rudolph interviewed some members of the cult and asked them why they joined the Hugo loyalist movement.

Harelipped Abbubakar's misery was compounded when he lost both legs during an encounter between government troops and Muslim rebels. He left the heartland of the Muslim rebellion in the south, known as Oloj, Ulus, and was presented to President Hugo by Muslim leaders when they made a pact to help him work for peace among Muslims and Christians.

Abbubakar was hosted by the First Couple. The First Lady brought in a plastic surgeon who performed surgery to fix his facial abnormality. She also provided him with a pair of artificial limbs.

When a radio commentator received threats from the Pink Tiger for airing his telephone conversations with the exiled president and the First Lady, Abbubakar was in the capital. He joined the Hugo loyalists who were encamped in the compound of Channel 8 to protect the commentator. Abbubakar was also in the Institute of Tourism when the speaker opened a rump session of parliament in defiance of the revolutionary government.

From there he encamped himself with the Hugo loyalists in front of the Gringolandia embassy to press for the return of the legally elected president. He joined the cult because its leader, the Reverend Manes, was a Hugo loyalist.

Juanito, a street vendor of *taho*, a concoction of ground soy beans topped with *muscovado,* related to Rudolph how he became a Hugo fanatic.

One afternoon, the First Lady's entourage passed by. Her limousine came to a sudden stop at the street corner where he was selling his brew. She was waving her handkerchief at him. She was so sparklingly clean, and he was smelling of grime and dirt, having gone without a bath for days.

He turned his back, feeling totally unprepared to deal with what he thought was a mirage. Two men in suits asked him to board their SUV and to bring along what he was selling. They drove him to the palace. He thought the worst, like being ordered salvaged by the First Lady, especially in light of the canard that priests and nuns working in depressed areas had been spreading in his neighborhood: that plans were afoot to eliminate squatters like him to rid the capital of eyesores.

"First Lady," he knelt down before her, "have pity on me. I haven't had a bath for days because there was no water and soap. My wife has been bedridden for days. She needs a heart bypass and I've got no money to buy soap or anything. I have to peddle *taho* because she needs medicines."

The First Lady told him to rise.

"Where is your *taho*?"

"I've sold everything."

"I just wanted to buy some. Next time, make more."

The First Lady gave him some money, enough to buy a supply of *taho* for the whole year. She also gave him dozens of sweet-scented soap. She had his wife fetched. She sponsored her heart bypass operation.

When the First Couple was abducted by the Gringolanders, Juanito's wife died of grief. Juanito met the Reverend Manes during the rump session of parliament. Right then and there he became a member of the cult. It was a parody of the Roman Catholic Church, but he did not know any difference. All that mattered to him was the chance to pray to God for the return of the Hugos, which at least this strange group was doing 24/7.

After a simple supper of rice and fish, the Reverend Manes brought Rudolph to his office and told him his story. Pelagio Manes once aspired to be a priest, having been a member of the Men's Guard of Honor of the Blessed Sacrament.

After a year, tired of the dysfunctional priests who seemed bent on making Islas e Islotes a theocracy, he left the seminary and was accepted in another one run by the Jesuits. In his second year of philosophy, while strolling on seminary grounds, he met a man who introduced himself as Ingkong. To Pelagio, Ingkong revealed his plan to make the seminarian part of his plan for world peace, progress and prosperity.

He told him time would come when servants of God would abandon their calling in favor of profanity and unholy activities. Ingkong appeared to be glowing.

The seminarian tried to touch the body of the old man to feel if he was real, but before he could, Ingkong had vanished into thin air.

From then on, Ingkong would appear to the young seminarian in visions. Sister Piedad, the mother of Pelagio, was given special powers by Ingkong. She received the gift to heal people. She levitated while praying. Her followers venerated Sister Piedad as a messenger from heaven.

Sister Piedad set aside fifty acres of land in Paga for cult members. She and her followers wanted to purify Christianity. They dressed themselves as priests and nuns.

Pelagio faced a dilemma. He was not sure whether his visions were inspired by God or by the Devil. His gifts of foretelling events tormented him. He left the seminary. Soon he had a jewelry store, a hair salon, a tailoring shop, a gym and a barber shop. When tourism boomed, he moonlighted as tourist guide. He got married. His wife bore him three daughters.

The man who was once devoted to the Blessed Sacrament was not satisfied with his life. He lived with paramours. He dreamed of his seminary days. In one of his dreams he was told by the old man to become a priest.

The village of Paga became some sort of a New Jerusalem for Sister Piedad, her son the Reverend Pelagio Manes and their followers. The Archbishop denounced the cult and declared its members apostates. Pelagio made a thorough soul-searching. He decided to go back to the seminary. The Roman Catholic Church could never take him back as a seminarian, let alone ordain him a priest.

But Pelagio believed in his dreams as divine manifestations. No power in heaven or on earth could prevent him from becoming a priest. He gave up everything and entered the seminary of the Ecumenical Catholic Church. There he had a place. He was ordained a priest, and the bishop sent him to Paga as pastor of Holy Trinity Church.

"Archbishop Khoneimo," the Reverend Manes said, "presumes too much. He has no jurisdiction over me. He must remember that Islas e Islotes has no official state religion."

Escorted by some members of the cult, Jessie and Georgina joined the Reverend Manes and Rudolph. A beautiful young woman garbed as a nun caught Rudolph's attention.

"She's from Cipac," the Reverend Manes said. "Her name's Tess Segismundo."

The young woman smiled, but there was sadness in her eyes.

# CHAPTER IX

# Between the Temple
# and the Altar

FATHER DEROVERE TIBURRON WAS BESIDE himself with excitement for his afternoon coffee session with Archbishop Khoneimo. He would miss *Ollantay*, his favorite afternoon *telenovela*, which he religiously followed inside his room, but he knew his priorities. His appointment with His Grace could not be postponed. The upstart Morán must be stopped. The necessary dossier had been provided to him by Colonel Reynaldo Garci, a human rights violator during the martial law period of Islas e Islotes and now a spy for the Girlie revolutionary government.

Since lately, Father Tiburron had managed the affairs of the parish of Extramuros without consulting his parochial vicars. He attended all meetings of parish priests and parochial vicars without bringing his assistants along with him. He adopted the "new accounting" which authorized parish priests, including the religious, to keep personal funds. They were also obliged to surrender a great portion of the parish funds to the chancery without consulting the community. He made it clear to the friars that his tenure as parish priest depended on the Archbishop, not on his religious superiors. Archbishop Khoneimo, he indicated, wanted him to stay as parish priest. The regional superior indefinitely postponed the reshuffling of the friars in Extramuros.

⟨✦⟩

Without the accord of the community, Father Tiburron took in Mistica Macbeth, a Gringolander divorcée who was prevailed upon to stay in Islas e Islotes by the friar.

Mistica was a single parent to a blonde boy, Wayne Junior, by her husband Wayne who had divorced her because he could not afford to raise a family. Out of "pure charity," as Father Tiburron would insist again and again for the benefit of the incredulous, a big chunk of his discretionary funds went to the education of the Wayne kid. The boy treated the monastery as his playground. Once, while running and yelling around the cloisters, "chasing the Indians," he was asked by Father Gordo who he was and he answered: "Father T is my father." Father Gordo chuckled, very much amused that the boy had a Father T for his father.

Mistica Macbeth was a scatterbrain but she was a very shrewd businesswoman. Father Tiburron found it fit to assign her to handle wedding receptions and videos. She could be completely trusted by Father Tiburron who had made it clear to her that her whole life depended on him, that she was accountable to him alone and to no one else. His wish was her command.

The week before, Father Tiburron performed a sham church wedding between his sister and a European Union national — for what purpose nobody really knew. Some personnel at the parish office surmised that it might have been for the sake of appearances. Since the rites were performed in a real church and presided over by a real priest, people that Father Tiburron's family was trying to impress through pictures of the church wedding posted in one of those social media sites would not know the difference.

Father Tiburron's mother was a very simple woman, guileless even, but her lack of education made her a little bit of a loose cannon. She had started telling Mistica Macbeth that back in their hometown, her daughter was very much married to a good-for-nothing alcoholic who could not get a steady job because, as she put it, "he's illiterate." She loudly praised and blessed God for giving her daughter another chance. Alarmed over the possible repercussions of the old woman's rather startling revelation, she wanted to protect Father Tiburron. She kept the old woman by her side and politely asked her to keep her mouth zipped, although it was hard for the old woman to understand Mistica's regional English accent. Mistica remembered the saying "loose lips sink ships" and she kept a close eye on Father Tiburron's mother throughout the wedding proceedings.

◦⟨∅⟩◦

Mistica Macbeth occupied Father Tiburron's thoughts as he drove to Villa Sinpecado, the archbishop's palace. He smiled with a sense of fulfillment. He had been irreproachable as Wayne Junior's surrogate father.

Whistling his favorite eucharistic hymn, "No más amor que el tuyo," the friar wistfully smiled as he craved for a promotion. It was very good to be a superior, but to be a bishop was even better. Lying secure on top of the passenger seat was his laptop bag, which contained a check he had written in favor of the Archbishop, a year's worth of salary for an ordinary government employee. Three pink plastic bags were also in the bag. They contained wads of dollar bills which he had not bothered to count because his three Marías had done it for him. They were "donations" from foreign nationals who wanted to be introduced by the Archbishop to President Girlie so they could invest in Islas e Islotes.

Unable to deliver groceries and other items to the Hugo loyalist freedom marchers, Gloria Singsonso decided to hitch a ride on a huge cargo truck driven by Colonel Garci. The undercover agent made her day by reminding her of her duty to go for the presidency of Islas e Islotes once an opportunity would arise. She was the daughter of Vedved Singsono, a former president soundly defeated by President Hugo in a landslide victory during the latter's first run for the presidency.

Both Gloria and the colonel always discussed politics whenever they got together. They had fun devising strategies on a number of ways she could grab the presidency so he could take charge of national defense and implement his torture program to wipe out the communist and the Muslim rebels.

Gloria was small in stature and stood less than five feet tall, but highly intelligent. She held two doctorates, or at least that was what she claimed: one in economics from Georgetown, the other in political science from the state university of Islas e Islotes.

It was shown later that she was less than truthful about her academic credentials. Investigative journalists examined her claims in the wake of a headline-grabbing scandal in the tech industry where some highly-paid CEOs got fired after it had been revealed that they had engaged in academic puffery. Their resumés were found to have shaded the truth to enhance their image. It turned out Gloria had obtained only an undergraduate economics degree from Georgetown, not a doctorate.

She was extremely short in stature even in a country whose general population was vertically challenged. She could never be capable of creating a stir nor be considered a threat to anyone if she ever entered a room full of total strangers. Her skill as a public speaker was below par, but her prowess to generate funds was second to none. Meanwhile, she was getting to be a byword among squatters. She gave them a steady supply of canned foods, used clothing and free medicines, courtesy of friends and relatives as well as relief and charitable institutions from abroad.

Lately, Gloria had established her own squatters' colony made up mainly of Hugo loyalists. Some lived under bridges, others on trees and still others on improvised cardboard houses near river banks that caused massive flooding in the metropolis during torrential rains because they had made the rivers a garbage bin of non-biogradable materials as well as a funnel for human wastes. Over the years, squatters had also effectively made the waterways toxic for various species of fish that used to thrive there decades ago. A great number settled in dump sites which they called "Smoky Empire." Gloria Singsonso visited them regularly, showering them with freebies. She had them registered as voters and stored their names in an extensive database of potential flying voters.

After the defeat of her father by Hugo, the Singsonsos did what every Islas e Islotes inhabitant adept in the art of survival in a country of active volcanoes, earthquakes, typhoons and floods would do: adapt to the changing times. In the case of the Singsonsos, this meant changing political colors like chameleons in the rainforests. The Singsonso matriarch, Doña Evita, one of the richest women of Islas e Islotes — her wealth no doubt being the primary factor that carried her husband to the pinnacle of political power — remained aloof but civil to the First Lady. On her sixtieth birthday, she signed her last will and testament naming, among many other institutions, Nobedlam Youth Drug Rehabilitation Center as one of her beneficiaries.

As its name suggested, Nobedlam Drug Rehabilitation Center for the Youth was an institution for young people, the "fair hope of the fatherland," so that no matter how hard they had fallen into drug abuse, they could still be cured of their drug addiction and made whole again to rejoin society.

Robby Gabone was fresh from receiving a citation from Montesini, signed by its school directress and high school principal Sister Bruhilda, lauding him for his wisdom in bringing worldwide attention to Islas e Islotes with his Palace Tour. Right after the departure of the Hugos to Nuncamuere, Robby brought any interested foreign correspondents to the palace, showing them the opulent lifestyle of the Hugos before their exile. The boudoir of the First Lady was opened for all curiosity-seekers to gawk at. Her seven thousand seven hundred seventy-seven pairs of shoes were exhibited for them to count until they got lost in the numbers. Robby's project surpassed all expectations. A news magazine published in Gringolandia gleefully awarded the dubious title to the First Lady as "the greediest mortal to ever walk the face of the earth after Genghis Khan."

Robby Gabone knew the ins and outs of the palace. When Hugo was elected president, he was a regular palace habitué. He himself was a byword among society matrons and *colegialas* from exclusive schools, known to every radio listener as Father Rob, the priest with a baritone voice that made their hearts beat faster and a television presence that glued them to their TV sets every Sunday evening, from ten to midnight, without fail. Even in their sick beds, they would call Father Rob and his infectious laughter could heal them.

Then the idea of helping drug-addicted youths hit Father Rob. In a matter of three months a one hundred-acre piece of property, dotted with cypresses, fire trees, firs, evergreens and weeping willows was donated by Doña Tiriring Ginuo, a flamboyant widowed millionaire hooked to her ballroom dancing instructor. She was already ninety-three years of age, but she looked only like thirty-five, thanks to her regular beauty regimen that included botox injections and trips to Germany where she was said to have taken advantage of the latest advances in stem cell therapy.

In a powerful display of anal-retentiveness, she boldly announced that she was marrying her twenty-nine-year-old dance instructor despite strong opposition from her family. The whole clan naturally objected to the May-December affair and suspected the dance instructor of manipulating the senior citizen so that he could inherit her wealth. The old woman fell ill from all the stress created by the incessant chatter around her planned marriage, not only by her family but by the talking heads on radio and on television, not to mention the rags. Father Rob was summoned to her hospital bed. The old woman pleaded with him to perform a miracle on her children so that they would accede to her wishes. Father Rob succeeded in persuading the children to respect her decision. She and her favorite dance instructor were married by Father Rob in Santa Lucia church, and the lavish event was instantly hailed by the press as the wedding of the century. The groom was made to sign, before he was asked to kiss the bride, a pre-nuptial agreement that entitled him to only ten million pesos of his wife's wealth, a chalet in the mountain resort town of Olopitna and nothing else.

༄

With Father Rob at the helm, Nobedlam became a home away from home for drug-addicted boys and girls. Under the watch of Father Rob, rehab residents heard Mass daily, confessed their sins once a month, exercised every day and learned a variety of skills from carpentry to computer repair and farming. They took turns in cooking and in keeping the place clean. They did their own laundry. Every Sunday evening, right after dinner at seven, they had Bible sharing.

Each resident was required to cultivate a vegetable plot that grew vegetables and root crops. They also maintained a poultry farm and a piggery. They were enrolled in a home study program following the syllabus drawn for that purpose by Sister Bruhilda and her fellow nuns at Montesini.

Father Rob wrote a syndicated advice column titled *Dear Father Rob*, hosted a daily radio program called *Father Rob*

*Needs You*, which was targeted at wayward and drug-addicted youths, and a late-night TV show dubbed *Why, Father Rob?* The latter drew lonely society matrons and dreamy and conflicted schoolgirls who poured out their souls to him Sundays from ten to twelve midnight.

Siboney was sixteen years old when she got enamored with Father Rob. She placed numerous calls under assumed names every night, sent him radio greetings every morning and spent nights and days collecting clippings of the celebrity priest. She could not have enough of him. Finally she devised a ruse so that she could be with him forever. She started taking drugs, making sure her parents got wind of it. They sent her to Nobedlam.

Four months later Father Rob was reportedly missing. His fans trooped to the radio and the TV stations that employed him as a talent and angrily demanded for answers on his disappearance. Some theorized that he was kidnapped by the rebels. Others thought he was abducted by the military. His religious superiors neither confirmed nor denied that he was missing. They nixed all interviews.

⁓

One morning, all the broadsheets and all the tabloids bannered similar headlines carrying the same story: "Father Robby Leaves Priesthood (To Get Married)." In a television talk show that night, gossip queen Inday Dimayacyac revealed that from then on Father Rob wanted to be known as Robby Gabone, happily married to Siboney Warns, a sixteen-year-old former resident of Nobedlam Drug Rehabilitation Center.

Father Rob's legion of followers went into deep mourning. "Why, Father Rob?" they asked in unison like a choir of grieving angels. A month later, Mr. and Mrs. Robby Gabone were always photographed with the First Lady, many times alongside Amparo, the international beauty title holder. Gloria discreetly chose to stay in the background, just listening and learning everything she could about politics. The Singsonso sisters became the flavor of the year for the First Lady whose preferences among her favored ones seemed always evolving and changing like the moods of the voters and the direction of the wind in these islands and islets of eternal summers.

Aside from her beauty, Gloria's sister Amparo was known not only for her intelligence but also for her wit. Sent to represent her country in an international beauty contest, she was asked a naughty question by an interviewer in an attempt to test her poise: "What is the euphemism for the male reproductive organ in your country?"

"Gossip?"

*"I beg your pardon?"* the interviewer thought she did not understand the question.

"Gossip," she repeated.

"Why?"

"Because, in my country," Amparo said, "it passes from mouth to mouth."

Her wit traveled by word of mouth and even long after she had relinquished her beauty crown, "gossip" became part and parcel of her fame as a beauty queen.

Gringolandia Ambassador to Islas e Islotes Mitzell Arcabus got smitten with Amparo. The feeling was mutual. In a party hosted by the First Lady to welcome the new ambassador, Gloria draped a lei of Arabian jasmine flowers around the ambassador's neck. He asked her to dance. While they were dancing

cheek to cheek to the tune of "Bésame mucho," they looked
into each other's eyes. That was all it took for them to discover
that they were hopelessly in love with each other.

They were very much married, she with a car racing cham-
pion and he with a nosy termagant who wrapped him around
her finger. The adage that everything is fair in love and in war
became an excuse for the pair to engage in adultery. Borders
were trespassed as boundaries were removed. Their mutual lust
for each other was all that mattered. They could not really call
it love. Neither of them had the courage to be seen holding
hands in public nor walking alone together. Their need was so
urgent that when they made love, they spent no time remov-
ing their clothes. They often met in holes and corners and had
sex between practice sessions at the clubhouse of the tennis
association where they were both looked up to as VIPs — he
as honorary president and she as muse. Gloria was the secret
courier for their coded messages to each other.

Then Georgie Bullock, whose family owned the debt-
ridden Brewlink Corporation which was under heavy pressure
from its creditor Gringolandia Bank, became secretary of state
of Gringolandia. Hendelson, the ambassador's twin brother,
happened to be the president of Gringolandia Bank. The first
thing Bullock did when his nomination was confirmed was
to invite the ambassador to his yacht. With only the flying
seagulls as disinterested witnesses to their confidential meeting, Secretary Georgie Bullock offered Mitzell Arbacus the position of deputy secretary of state.

The news of the ambassador's promotion to the state department was met by the First Lady with ebullience and ex-
hilaration. Ambassador Arbacus had never been absent in
any party she hosted in the palace. Both Amparo and Gloria

always saw to that. She asked Amparo to help her organize a send-off party for the ambassador around the theme of "I Shall Return."

Little did the lovers know that the ambassador's wife had gotten wind of their affair. Being a jealous wife, she had always put the ambassador under surveillance. Not only that. She had both of their email accounts hacked. She was able to decipher the coded messages of her husband to his mistress as well as the ones of the mistress who, much to her surprise, turned out to be the beauty queen, a regular companion of the First Lady in many of her social functions.

Upon learning that Amparo had a hand in organizing the farewell party for her husband, she called up the First Lady and threatened to boycott the party if her husband's paramour's name would not be expunged from the guest list. She likewise wrote a letter. Her demand was granted. Amparo and Gloria were conspicuously absent in the party.

Mitzell Arbacus flew into a rage when the party ended. As he descended the palace stairs, half sober and half drunk, he ominously told the First Lady: "I'm going to the state department where all decisions are made. You'll hear more from me."

Robby Gabone smilingly welcomed Gloria and Colonel Garci with open arms. He whistled three times. Immediately three male residents got out of their cubicles and stood at attention before him to receive orders. He snapped a finger at the direction of Gloria's truckload of goods for Nobedlam and in a matter of seconds the three started unloading the crates and boxes.

"Megan, what's wrong, *hija?*" Megan's mother bellowed

and rushed to the teenager before she could remove the last strap of her clothing. Megan pushed her aside and seductively posed for Robby's benefit. She was now wearing nothing but her thongs and even these she removed with the expertise of a stripteaser. Soaked in perspiration, Robby turned pale and was beside himself. He stood there immobile by this sudden turn of events and unable to think, except to wait for her next move. Siboney pushed her husband aside and ordered the three young residents out of Megan's sight, telling them to hurry with their work of unloading the truck. Gloria picked up Megan's clothes on the floor and handed them to her mother who lost no time in covering the young woman's nakedness. Siboney jabbed the girl's arm with an injection and within seconds she was curling on her bed like a fetus in its mother's womb. All the while, unknown to them, the colonel was secretly recording the scene with his cellphone pretending to dial a number.

Feeling more threatened than scared, Siboney nervously covered the eyes of her husband with both her hands. Siboney vividly remembered her first night in Nobedlam. She was the same age as Megan, but very daring. She did not have to suffer a nervous breakdown to get what she wanted. She always got what she wanted because she worked for it, no matter what the cost.

She made her moves that night. Propelled by a primal urge, she went straight to the office of her priest idol, Father Rob, without bothering to knock. Father Rob had to blink his eyes several times to be sure that she was not an apparition. Siboney was standing before him, wearing nothing but her smile. Suddenly he was paper, she was fire, and their raging desire a mighty wind. He ceased to be a fantasy that very moment. He slid back to being a mere mortal, with a raging desire that was all at once achingly potent and unbridled. He was paper, she was fire, and their fiery passion became an untamable conflagration that consumed them both. They were virgins, but the ritual they performed required no practice. Pleasure, not experience, was all that mattered. At first he was a unicorn that then turned into a stallion, pinning her to the space that kept revolving with his every move. Then he grew wings and rode her to the heights of ecstasy until both of them shuddered and burst with the explosions and implosions of the stars.

After doing it two more times that same night, Siboney told the priest that she was only sixteen and still a minor. The priest at first sighed deeply and was lost in his own thoughts. Before heading to his chalet he told her that he would marry her. She was not convinced. She hastily put on her clothes and followed him to his bedroom and refused to leave. That morning they were missing from Nobedlam, hiding in the family safe house.

A justice of the peace pronounced them husband and wife. When the priest was asked to kiss his bride, he was crying, his tears streaming down his cheeks to his lips.

Gloria and Colonel Garci went back to their truck. They must deliver sacks of rice to Villa Sinpecado for the Archbishop's soup kitchen.

༺❧༻

Father Tiburron's car screeched to an abrupt halt. His eyeglasses fell due to the impact. His vision went blurred. He thanked his guardian angel when he found his eyeglasses resting on his lap intact and not broken.

He hurriedly opened his car to see whether he had run over someone because he had heard rustling noises. Thankfully, it was just a couple of playful cats that came from the newly renovated Islas e Islotes Hotel, a government-owned landmark.

That day, every hotel room was occupied. Reservations had been paid in advance for a week's stay. Restaurants, lounges and bars were packed. Prices of food and drinks were trebled and when some customers started complaining, they were told not to order anything if they could not afford it.

The first batch of squatters that Colonel Garci had trucked in did not have to worry about accommodation and food. They quietly pitched their red tents on hotel grounds outside its majestic Renaissance-style building. Every item they brought was in red. One tent was beautifully embossed with a scythe and anvil and a quarter moon. The eye-catching design did not escape the attention of Roy Gernale. He and his wife Coritha pointed this out to Father Morán.

Before the departure of the Hugos, Father Morán was a prison volunteer at the maximum security unit of the national penitentiary. Tired and sick of living a privileged life as a friar, he wanted to do something that would at least let him pass through the eye of a needle. Roy, being an elected village chairman, encouraged his constituents to donate chessboards and basketballs to the prisoners.

Father Tiburron found himself facing a multitude of squatters going in his direction. About a dozen heavily armed men in military fatigues were escorting them. Then he heard the familiar pro-Hugo chants amid the beating of deafening drums. People from every direction were headed toward the hotel. Instinctively, he reached for his cell phone.

⁂

*"Goddamit!"*

The expletive that issued from his mouth was more of a cry. His phone was missing as well as his wallet.

He felt lost among the Hugo loyalists whom he considered barbarians. Frightened, he ran back to his car. He had forgotten to close the door in his haste to see if he had hit someone. His laptop bag with the Morán dossier in it was gone! The three pink plastic bags with wads of dollars in them were all gone, too. He went inside his car, slammed the door, collapsed himself on the driver's seat and started banging his head against the steering wheel.

# CHAPTER X

# The Called
# and the Chosen

AT EXACTLY SEVEN O'CLOCK in the evening, Father Rubio softly rang the bell, knowing that the rest of the six other friars of Extramuros were already there in their respective places at the round table waiting for him. He briskly strode to the dining room. Sure, indeed, they were all there chatting and exchanging pleasantries, totally relaxed, waiting for him. For reasons only he knew, Father Tiburron was not around for dinner. Father Gordo was on vacation. Judging from the expression on everyone's faces, Father Rubio anticipated dinner to be a happier time than usual. He said the grace in Latin after which he opened a bottle of red rioja wine brought by Father Hernández when he came back from vacation last year.

It was a simple dinner of garlic soup, *galunggong*, rice and bread, but the absence of two friars transformed it into a sumptuous agape of brotherhood and friendship. Camaraderie and sharing were on display, making it a pleasant task for those concerned to live together as a religious family united in harmony under one roof. Father Rubio opened a box of honey-sweetened fig bars, sent by a former student way back in the university when he was assigned there as comptroller. The student, now a civil engineer, had landed a lucrative job with a British firm in Dubai and sent him twelve boxes of the confections, enough to last for a year.

Fray Ferrer lost his reticence and recited some lines from San Juan de la Cruz whose *Dark Night of the Soul* in its original Spanish version was the only book he found worth keeping in his bookshelf, sandwiched between the Jerusalem Bible and *Ripley's Believe It or Not.* He waxed nostalgic over the pre-Vatican II lifestyle when for a seminarian to look outside the window was a very grave offense and therefore enough reason for dismissal. Their Father Master, he said, spoke in parables like Jesus Christ. Every time he talked about the "tempest in the harbor," he would send them for a walk at Piniar Park. They went there in their white religious habit and won the admiration of the devout but turned off pickpockets who derisively heckled them "whited sepulchers" and told them to go back to the monastery. By the time they got back to their dormitory that could accommodate thirty single beds, someone's bed had been removed. The bed's occupant had been told to leave.

❦

Why were monasteries filled with aspirants in those days? The friars wondered among themselves but got no answer. In those days, obedience was all. The aspirant could be ordered by the Prior to plant a tree upside down. He must have to carry out the order without question, lest he would be sent home. Had he been commanded by the Prior to jump out of the window, Fray Ferrer said he would have complied without hesitation.

The voice of the superior was the voice of God. It was the duty of every subject to obey. A superior could never be wrong just as God could never be wrong.

They had a live-in lay driver in the monastery, Fray Ferrer also recalled, who would sneak out some nights to join singing contests. With the approval of the Prior, then choir master Father Daniel encouraged him to make use of his gift. Father Daniel in turn was told by the Prior to teach the singing driver advanced lessons in music *gratis et amore*. His training paid off for Amado the driver soon won the championship of a national singing competition. Upon winning, he was offered on the spot to co-host the same Sunday TV talent show that conducted the competition, leaving the friars without a driver. To solve the problem, Derovere Tiburron volunteered himself to be the dedicated driver of the monastery. The friars blessed God for they needed him to run errands. They freed the nuns from further shouldering his seminary expenses by sponsoring his studies for the priesthood themselves even if in those days' standard, he was a little old to be numbered among teenage aspirants.

Father Bolero was unusually talkative. He told a lot of funny anecdotes which made Father Merino laugh at every turn. Father Morán shared with them his experiences as volunteer in the maximum security unit of the national penitentiary. Father Mayo divulged how it was to live in a Muslim-dominated region of Islas e Islotes. Father Hernández told them his personal, oftentimes hilarious, misadventures upon his arrival, in black habit, in the tropical islands.

Before saying the thanksgiving prayer at dinner's end, Father Rubio proposed that they play the card game *brisca* which did not limit the number of participants. The proposal was heartily seconded. Each one carrying a chair, the seven friars proceeded to the recreation room.

The friars were in the middle of the game when they heard hurried footsteps and loud opening and closing of doors. A loud banging of door leading to their cloister led Father Bolero to make a clown of himself by jumping like a frog to the delight of everybody. Even Father Merino convulsed with laughter. During dinner, Father Bolero had become like a son to him, or a nephew, or even a mischievous waif who needed guidance and support because he had just been ordained.

It was only Father Tiburron in a cranky mood as usual. By the kind of noises he created, he seemed to be to other friars like a skunk intruder in a barbecue party of friends. Father Tiburron resented the fact that nobody acknowledged his presence. He felt like a rejected toy at a rummage sale for toddlers. To register his displeasure, he made his presence felt by tapping the unbreakable glass partition that separated the recreation room and the corridor.

When still nobody paid any attention, he brusquely opened the translucent fiberglass door. He needed a scapegoat for the collective transgressions of the friars against him. He looked at the direction of Father Morán and imperiously ordered: "Hey, come here! You!" He stared hard, looking very peeved, at the direction of Father Morán.

Father Mayo whispered to Father Morán that Father Tiburron was calling him. Angered by the manner he was rudely interrupted in the middle of a game and discourteously summoned, he continued playing.

Father Tiburron reached his boiling point. He furiously stormed into the recreation room holding a book of weddings which he waved for everyone to see. After whacking a coffee table book with what he was holding, he stood before Father Morán and started berating him like a child who had stolen his security blanket and must be punished.

"You, why did you authorize this Martínez to officiate at tomorrow's wedding? He's banned from performing any wedding ceremony here. I've banned him from doing anything here in *my* parish."

Father Yul Martínez was an archdiocesan priest whose huge following among benefactors and donors had endeared him to the Archbishop who started calling him as "my personal mascot." According to a coterie of gossiping pious ladies who provided information to Father Tiburron on the daily happenings in the parish, Father Martínez looked like the extraterrestrial character in a sci-fi movie, so they called him Father E.T.

It was not the priest's barely five feet E.T. persona that got the goat of Father Tiburron. Rather, it was the glib-talking priest's flair and skill to make friends with millionaires that made the inarticulate friar green with envy. Father Martínez was requested to officiate at church weddings every day in different churches within the archdiocese. Completely apolitical, he had endeared himself to the Archbishop who personally praised him for his ability to raise funds and acknowledged his regular contribution to the soup kitchen project. The pious ladies had also told Father Tiburron, their source undisclosed, that Father E.T. was being considered by the Archbishop for promotion to the bishopric because he wanted him to be his auxiliary bishop.

Father Morán politely replied: "He had a letter of endorsement from the Vicar General. It would be stupid of me to ignore that letter of endorsement. It was not only an endorsement. It was an order."

"Stupid? *Oh, yes? Stupid!* You have the bad habit of calling everybody here stupid! Stupid is the only word you know to describe everyone of us here! You consider anyone other than yourself stupid! That's why everyone in the parish hates you. Do you think only you have the monopoly of wisdom?"

"But Father Martínez is also a priest!"

"Are you raising your voice at me? How dare you raise your voice at me! You want to fight?" Father Tiburron stumped off the recreation room, clenched his fists and challenged Father Morán to get out of the room and fight.

The friars could not believe what they were seeing, let alone what they were hearing from their Prior.

"Come now, Father Prior," the younger friar said, "did we finish philosophy and theology just to become savages? If you want it badly, then go box yourself."

"Why were you ordained? You shouldn't have been ordained priest!"

"And you with a missing finger and two black votes to block your profession, why were you ordained? Why do you question my being ordained? Are you God?"

"Stop going to the office, you less than human scum of the earth! I'll have your name removed as parochial vicar."

"Don't you want any competition? Is it my fault that I'm more intelligent and more charming than you are? The ordinary appointed me parochial vicar, the same ordinary who appointed you pastor. You're not a bishop. You're only a friar. Just like me."

The sharp retort jolted him back to reality that he was not, indeed, a bishop. Father Tiburron whined in agony: "I don't want to be superior anymore. I'm tired...but...the Archbishop."

"Then why the hell don't you resign? Resign, and our life in the monastery would be heaven, not the kind of purgatory that you want to impose."

At this juncture, the friars gathered around the two men to pacify them. It was then that Father Morán noticed the stitches on the Prior's head covered by his thick, dark locks. His brown temple appeared a little swollen. He had bloodshot eyes.

⁙

Momentarily transported back by his memory to the past, Father Morán's recollection settled at times past in the Guadalupana novitiate.

Shentavim Circus put up that summer a three-day carnival in Guadalupana church compound. After dinner, the novices were allowed by Father Hernández, in the spirit of the Second Vatican Council, to join the crowd and have some fun and be one with the people. They were given tickets to watch every show the circus offered. One night he went to what appeared to be a special added attraction of two male monkeys chasing each other and having a wrestling match against each other. The monkeys jumped with joy at being stared at and cheered to victory. They were vying for the attention of the female monkey who was in another cage. Whoever would win in the wrestling match would be transferred to the cage of the female monkey, leaving the loser alone in the other cage.

His co-novice, Roman Barriga — later he asked for a regency but never came back — saw the two wrestling monkeys showing off their prowess. He coaxed them to shake hands but they scratched and bit his left forearm. He grabbed a twig and made a show of whipping the two monkeys with it. The two scared animals desperately and futilely tried to escape from the cage. They ended up hugging each other when they instinctively realized that they only had each other. After that, not even the trainer could make them fight.

And here he was, quarreling with his Prior for nothing. His Prior bullied him because he was a loyalist sympathizer, not a rabid follower of the Girlie regime. Were they not both guilty of being untrue to their vows as religious and their profession as priests, as men of God? They were supposed to forgive, not to condemn. To lead people to heaven, not to send them to hell. By getting involved in politics, they divided the people.

What happened to his idea of leaving the world to make it better? Was the world much better now because he was so obsessed with helping whom he considered, according to his own personal judgment, the destitute, the exiled and the oppressed? Why would he have to fight his Prior or even Archbishop Khoneimo for doing the same? They were in the same boat but working in different directions, the reason the boat could not reach their salvific goal. Were not the exiled, the destitute and the oppressed already promised beatitude if they accepted their fate and suffered in solidarity with their avowed Redeemer and Savior who their faith taught them died blameless to save the world to the point of dying the most ignominious death which was death on the cross?

In his eyes, Father Tiburron had become one with the destitute, the exiled and the oppressed because he had failed to understand his calling. He, too, like Father Tiburron, his brother in the habit, had detoured from his calling. Those who betrayed their calling were Judas priests. If he and Father Tiburron would not give up their biases, would they not both end up as Judas priests?

Father Morán got teary-eyed and remorseful as compunction pricked his innermost conscience. Father Tiburron ceased to be an enemy but a brother, a friend, a companion in this life's journey, standing side by side with him.

"We're all sinners and we both sinned," Father Morán softly said as he hugged Father Tiburron. "We're brothers no matter what. Things like this happen because we're brothers. Let's forgive each other and forget what happened tonight. We've been brothers. Like it or not we'll always be brothers."

The older friar could not bring himself to hug Father Morán. What had led him to bully and run after the younger friars but his aspiring to be what he could not be. He was guilty of envy and jealousy. He was unhappy if others succeeded and felt happy if they failed.

⟡

Before Father Morán there were several other victims of his misguided ambition, his envy and his jealousy. When they were aspirants, he was the oldest so he was tasked to help the Father Master in forming the younger seminarians. Instead of helping them, he put them down. Vic Dunggo was the first victim. He did not like him because he could drive better and not a finger of his was missing.

Vic left the monastery and was ordained a diocesan priest after the Father Master had advised him to leave as a result of Fray Tiburron's devious schemes that put Vic in a bad light. Later the Father Master realized that Fray Tiburron had fed him false information regarding the conduct of his fellow seminarians and he became angry at the latter's machinations. He cast a black vote in due time to block Fray Tiburron's profession. Three black votes were needed to expel Fray Tiburron. His black vote and that of another formator fell short, but enough to delay the process until a compromise was reached.

Then there was Father Leonilo who recently passed away a broken man from all the stress he had to go through with Father Tiburron's constant harassment. He recruited him thinking he could be his pawn but when Father Leonilo showed some independence, Father Tiburron did his best to ostracize him. Father Trinity, on the other hand, simply fled to Australia after receiving anonymous death threats from Father Tiburron's politician friends who felt alluded to by Father Trinity's sermons. Only Father Morán was left standing among his targets.

"Don't resign. Nobody wants to be in your shoes," Father Morán told Father Tiburron.

"You can stay as parochial vicar," the older friar responded as he turned his back and retreated to his room. In his mind, he could hardly wait for the moment when what he had planned with a corrupt military official in the Girlie government would finally bring Father Morán down to his knees and out of his way.

# CHAPTER XI

# Witnessing

HE HERETOFORE NAMELESS FEMALE radio block timer who called herself Happily Anonymous finally surfaced to see and to be seen by fellow Hugo loyalists. "Luz de los Cielos, at your service," she addressed in her lilting voice a throng of enraptured listeners who had gathered at the main entrance of Islas e Islotes Hotel to hang on to her every word. They were her avid followers. Twice each day, they tuned in to her, along with millions of other listeners throughout the country, from ten to twelve noon and from ten to twelve midnight.

"Beloved compatriots," she told her captive listeners, "our beloved president, the most intelligent in the whole world, and our beloved First Lady, the most beautiful in the universe, are now in Nuncamuere against their will. Our beloved Islas e Islotes is being occupied by Gringolandia green card holders who enjoy the support of foreign agents." At this, she started sobbing and her listeners sobbed with her. The throng had swelled into a crowd that eventually overflowed the compound of Islas e Islotes Hotel up to the main gate.

The officer-in-charge of the government-owned hotel did

not quite know how to react to the situation. For the first time since its total renovation before the departure of the Hugos, the hotel was fully booked. The lucky guests who were able to get a reservation did not hide the fact that they were Hugo loyalists. When regular rallyists commented that they did not look familiar, they would say: "Right. We're the eleventh-hour Hugo loyalists. We show ourselves when we're most needed. And we're not afraid."

They were right. Most of those fighting for the return of the Hugos came at the eleventh hour. They guffawed at the suggestion that they must have gone crazy because they were there when nobody called them to be there. At their own expense. Hugo cronies had saved themselves like rats jumping from a sinking ship, and many Red Ladies who benefited the most from the First Lady had flipped side by donning pink apparel and badmouthing the Hugos. They did not want to complicate their lives.

Luz de los Cielos had no love lost for the Hugo cronies and the ministers and the lawmakers who had deserted him. But now they were coming, swarming the hotel like locusts. She spotted them among her listeners.

"The scoundrels of Islas e Islotes made politics their last refuge. They fooled the people. They fooled the Hugos. They fooled you. They fooled me. They fooled us," she wailed.

The hotel officer-in-charge who did not want people to know his real identity quietly ordered security to bug the five-star hotel resort for evidence in a possible case of rebellion to be filed against the Hugo loyalist ringleaders. Every movement of Luz de los Cielos was closely monitored, her every word recorded.

"Some of them pronounce the word *'debris'* with an *'s,'*" she said. "That chihuahua wanted no other dogs in the palace other than himself. He was supposed to provide the people with what's good and true and beautiful. He was supposed to tell the truth. But he misled the president and the First Lady and what happened? Even our most beloved president, the most intelligent in the world, and our beloved First Lady, the most beautiful in the universe, lost their own credibility because of this scoundrel."

Luz de los Cielos seemed to have blacked out because she stopped for a few minutes. Comedian Abnoy Binsaya, attired as a Shaolin monk, offered her a glass of water, but she refused it. Instead, overwhelmed with a terrible feeling of grief and a sense of loss, she choked and wailed even louder like a paid mourner in a Chinese funeral.

Among those standing in front was Anita, the limbless boy now on a new wheelchair beside her. She completely identified herself with Luz de los Cielos. They were not there when the Hugos had Islas e Islotes to rule. Now that the Hugos were languishing in Nuncamuere and disgraced to the level of mere worms, the poor were there demanding that the Hugos be restored to their proper place.

Anita opened her faded red handbag and took out a red handkerchief. She gave it to Luz de los Cielos to wipe the tears in her eyes. She also took out a folded red fan from the same red handbag. Before she could give it to Luz de los Cielos, the block timer grabbed the fan from her and opened it. The crowd lustily cheered, clapping their hands as hard as possible.

Painted in water color on the red fan was President Hugo with the First Lady beside him. That kind of fan, on sale at the entrance gate of the hotel, was handcrafted by the inmates of the national penitentiary.

Comedian Abnoy Binsaya, this time attired as Sindbad the Sailor, glided in, waltzing from the lobby to the main entrance of the hotel. Midget action star Bling-bling servilely opened the door for him. He unceremoniously lifted Bling-bling and just as unceremoniously carried him on his back. Both were flashing the V-sign and urging the people to do the same. Luz de los Cielos fanned herself furiously for it was a hot, humid evening with the full moon serving as a beacon light from the sky that became a big dome studded with twinkling stars. Islas e Islotes Hotel, with all its obsolete fluorescent and incandescent and cutting-edge, light-emitting diode lights on, majestically shone like a palace for the microcosmos of those Hugo loyalists who were gathered there that night determined to bring the Hugos back.

*"Hu-go! Hu-go! Hu-go! Hu-go still!"*
*"Hu-go! Hu-go! Hu-go! Hu-go forever!"*

After a half-hour walk from the monastery, Father Morán reached Islas e Islotes Hotel. Luz de los Cielos was now lashing at the bad elements in the military, singling out the arrogant wife of the air force chief whose warped sense of entitlement had given the Hugos a black eye even among their allies in Gringolandia.

Father Morán was transported back to the historic church of Extramuros. He was the celebrant during the penultimate night of the novena Masses Prior to the celebration of the feast of Our Lady of Consolation and Cincture. That had been a tiresome day for him for he had just returned from his apostolate at the national penitentiary as a prison volunteer. The *hermana mayor* that year was the wife of the armed forces chief of Islas e Islotes, and she was running late. He could have started the Mass without her, but he decided to wait in deference to her as *hermana mayor*. When she finally arrived, he welcomed her at the entrance of the church and escorted her to a special seat reserved for her. He introduced her to the congregation and invited them to give her a round of applause for being so devoted to the Blessed Virgin Mary, who held a special place in their faith, he said, as the first among Christians for being the mother of humanity's Redeemer. The Mass went on very smoothly, and everybody later on was one in saying that the choir had put on a fine performance. After the Mass, the *hermana mayor* graciously looked for him.

"Anything you want for your apostolate, Father?" she asked. "I like your Mass. Can I be of help to you? I'm willing to give you what you need." She was handling what appeared to be a bulky envelope. He knew what would happen next if he did not say anything.

"My apostolate is with the prisoners. I know that not all who are sent to prison are guilty of a crime. Maybe you could use your clout with your husband to help some deserving inmates get out of prison."

"That's a holy thing to do, Father," she said, putting the bulky envelope inside her designer handbag. "I would really want to get in touch with you on this matter."

When he went up to his room to change into a Roman collar, he felt like he was on top of the world for, at last, he could tell some of the prisoners that he had started the ball rolling for their possible release. Judge Normita Medina, a very devout Catholic whose house was home to one of the twelve original replicas of the image of Our Lady of Fatima, was waiting for him downstairs. She was intrigued with his idea of helping falsely accused convicts get out of prison by providing them with free legal assistance. The judge herself was willing to offer pro bono legal advice and volunteered to recruit her colleagues to the cause.

The wife of the air force chief was inside the church, pacing back and forth. When she reached the pew where Judge Medina was praying, she angrily snarled at him: "Father, do you have a minute?"

"You want to confess? The confessional is there."

"You're not a priest!" she yelled. "Why did you tell her to help the prisoners? Is it our fault that people are in prison? Who's the superior here? I want to talk to him. The superior here should know this!"

She was totally shorn of any respect even for the fact that she was inside a sacred place. Father Morán was unable to immediately grasp what had possessed this woman to show such insolence and total disrespect. He was frozen and speechless where he stood, and yet a tremendous sense of peace took over his entire being.

He was prepared to be arrested. To go to prison for interceding for the innocent was for him a privilege.

"*Generala*," Judge Medina intervened. "Don't get angry. You might have a heart attack."

"Don't call me *Generala*!!!" she screamed and stormed off the church in a huff.

The elder sister of the woman apologized to everybody for the behavior of her sibling who, she said, was on the verge of a nervous breakdown. Father Morán silently prayed before the image of Our Lady of Consolation and Cincture. He could remember every word: "Dearest Mother, it's not me but my priesthood that was debased. I'm one hundred percent convinced that this regime is evil. Please let it fall."

Father Morán wryly smiled as he began to realize the irony of it all for himself. That by being one with the Hugo loyalists at Islas e Islotes Hotel at that moment, he was effectively revoking himself. Why was he there, at the eleventh hour, when nobody even invited him to come? Why was he there when his elder brother was a victim of martial law?

⸙

The ugly incident with the powerful wife of the air force chief had traumatized and even scared him a bit. After a sleepless night, the sun was just a glimmer when he started walking out the main monastery door. Without even taking his breakfast, he took the next bus to the penitentiary to spend an extra day of volunteer work there. In all his past visits, he had always something to bring to the inmates, but this time he brought nothing but his concern that he might be arrested for trying to intercede for them.

"This might be my last day as a free man," he said. "For all we know I might even join you if they sent me here."

Shane started bawling like a baby, a totally unexpected and unusual reaction from the most feared and longest held prisoner on death row. He had committed a lot of gruesome crimes but nothing could top the gory he perpetrated during a prison riot. He beheaded an opposing gang member with a rusty knife, carried his severed head dripping with blood around and played bowling with it. The rioting stopped when even the prisoners themselves were shell-shocked by what they had witnessed and fled the scene into the waiting arms of prison guards outside. Shane's gruesome antics in prison later became the basis of a movie that catapulted a then unknown action star Moammar Saddam to superstardom. When President Hugo abolished the death penalty, a public defender told Shane that his only hope of being released was a pardon from the president.

"Why don't you talk to the First Lady?" Shane wondered aloud. "Just try..." he trailed, embarrassed that he had been crying.

"Okay, Shane," he said.

"Pray to Maximillian Kolbe for his intercession. I hate that mad woman with all my heart and with all my mind, but for your sake and that of other prisoners, I'm willing to kneel down before her."

He wondered whether he was giving them false hopes. He found it very hard to be identified with a government he held responsible for the torture of his brother during martial law.

He was invited to have lunch with the prisoners. They ate with their bare hands, so he did the same. He observed Shane eating like a platypus and the sight made him almost throw up. The friar imagined the hardened criminal eating the severed head of his victim dripping with blood from the bloody hands of Shane. He found an excuse to get out of there fast.

⸙

He took the first cab to pass his way, which brought him to the bus station for the hour-long ride back to the capital. He got off at a bus stop near Piniar Park from where he started walking back to the monastery.

He was feeling very tired and ready for a hot bath when he noticed a limousine slowly following him and then stopping beside him just before he was about to cross a wide, tree-lined boulevard by Azucar Bay. The limo's back door opened and out came a beautiful woman with sunglasses. She looked at him with a wide smile on her face and extended her right hand for a handshake, acting as though she knew him like an old friend. The fast-moving events took him off his stride that he did not notice right away that they were not alone. In fact, they were being surrounded by well-dressed security escorts, sporting dark sunglasses and talking into Secret Service-style mouthpieces. A number of them did not leave the SUVs trailing the limo.

"The First Lady wants to invite you to come with her to discuss some projects you may be interested in," one of the stern-looking men gently told him.

"I'm a priest," he said.

"We need more religious people like you to get involved constructively in nation-building," the First Lady said.

"I just came from the penitentiary," he said. "I work there as prison volunteer."

"That's what we need," she said. "Not all of those in jail

are guilty. Some of them are falsely accused. President Hugo was in jail as a student. Falsely accused of killing the political adversary of his father."

⁂

Later batches of the various squatter groups that Colonel Garci had organized arrived at Islas e Islotes Hotel in trucks, buses and all sorts of motor vehicles. They unenthusiastically pitched red tents on a vacant lot outside the hotel compound as there was no more space for them inside. While the squatters were not pleased camping outside the hotel itself, Colonel Garci saw it as a small inconvenience. Despite the squatters' loud complaints about being denied the lavish surroundings of the hotel which they had never tasted in all their miserable lives, the military strategist in Colonel Garci paid no heed to them. He intended to use them as human shields for the Hugo loyalists holed up inside the hotel. He was a Girlie spy, but he couldn't refuse Gloria's plea for his help. He knew which side his bread was buttered on.

Although she never showed her face, Gloria saw to it that the squatters had everything they needed for what she expected to be a quick and decisive military takeover of the Girlie government. The brewing coup needed civilian support, and the people had to make a decision: they were either with the illegitimate regime of Madame Girlie Chichi Vda. de Almagro or with the legitimate president, Pacifico Hugo. They were either with us or against us. There was not any place for equivocation. Assorted foodstuffs, bottled water, first-aid kits, flashlights, blankets and other supplies were flowing into the area until the checkpoints did their job of stanching the flow.

"This is the palace of the poor," the squatters said to one another as they made themselves feel at home. "We're the reasons Islas e Islotes Hotel was renovated by the First Lady."

The sunny disposition that the inhabitants of Islas e Islotes put on constant display before the eyes of the world was only a facade that kept from view the true and rotten state of the unhappy nation. The people were always smiling whether they were happy, sad, annoyed, pleased, hungry, angry or for no reason at all. Whatever their state of mind, poverty was the handmaiden of the majority of the people, which rendered them vulnerable to politicians who exploited them for their own vested interests and personal aggrandizement.

That night people wore smiling faces. They were expecting something decisive to happen when the clock struck midnight. At the eleventh hour Vice President Chavezcu, running mate of President Hugo, was supposed to declare himself president *ad interim* until the Hugos' homecoming. They were expecting that, to coincide with the arrival of the freedom marchers later that night, the military would defect to their side.

"I've got something for you," Lieutenant Marfori whispered. Father Morán snapped out of his reverie and followed him outside the compound. They walked past the red tents of Colonel Garci's self-proclaimed Hugo loyalist sentinels. Father Morán was dismayed to see that checkpoints had been set up by the Girlie government around the hotel. They were being manned by what he thought were elements of the Pink Tiger, effectively denying any access to the area. He knew that the success of the whole enterprise depended on how many people the hotel and surrounding areas could muster to support the military if and when they moved.

But Roy Gernale assured the priest, "Don't worry for now. Those checkpoints are under the command of Lieutenant Marfori. You must come with us. You're being targeted. You can still save your priesthood in exile. Better one living coward than a thousand dead heroes."

Much to Father Morán's surprise, Ganymede was there with Roy. But he ignored his younger brother momentarily as he turned to Roy and said, "Why do you tell me this?"

"Here," Lieutenant Marfori handed Father Morán a folder. "Read as fast as you can. I'll give you only five minutes."

Under the light of the full moon he read the dossier that Father Tiburron had wanted to turn over to the Archbishop. It accused him, among other fabrications, of having sex with a minor, Megan Reynoso. The accusation was corroborated by a letter of Megan to his father general detailing their alleged daily sexual calisthenics that supposedly lasted a long nine months. They presented no police reports nor any concrete evidence, except some juicy recollections purportedly written by Megan herself on the alleged sexual encounters over a period of those months. Readers of smut magazines would easily recognize Megan's letter for what it was: a bad attempt at pornographic plagiarism. His accusers were not demanding for any compensation from Father Morán's religious order or from the Catholic Church itself. They made it clear in no uncertain terms, however, that their supposedly benign and altruistic goal was simply to keep him away from any public ministry so that he could do no more harm to anyone — man, woman or child.

⁂

Islas e Islotes was notorious for the rapacity of some individuals to come out of nowhere to bear false witness in exchange for the right amount of money or for political favors. They smiled often to hide a vindictive nature. Some pious souls in Islas e Islotes would not hesitate to put God in their soup just to get even with someone who had hurt them. They had done that to the son of a senator who was found innocent of the crimes of rape and murder after having languished in jail for ten years. Father Tiburron had not evidently forgiven him. He was all smiles in public, but the slanderous and false accusations spoke for themselves.

"At least it's not a boy that they're accusing you of having sexual liaisons with," Ganymede comforted his brother.

"Everything is absurd," Father Morán replied.

"President Hugo is waiting for you there. He needs a priest because he won't live long," Roy Gernale said as he showed Father Morán two round-trip plane tickets to Nuncamuere.

"Ganymede," Father Morán told his youngest sibling, "no matter what happens, get a college degree."

"He can work for me and study. You don't have to worry about him. He looks successful. He'll succeed," Roy said.

⁂

The unnerving wail of sirens sounded seconds after the metropolis had been deliberately plunged into total darkness. The blackout extinguished every single light over a wide swath of city neighborhoods. Lieutenant Marfori raised the volume of his portable radio for some news.

"The freedom march has been broken and dispersed," the broadcaster excitedly announced. "The ringleader only known as Jessie because he refuses to disclose his last name has been arrested together with all his cohorts who also refuse to disclose their identities. A pregnant young woman only known as Georgina has been rushed to the hospital. She's unable to talk and is in critical condition. A fake nun identified only as Tess belonging to a cult condemned by Archbishop Khoneimo has escaped. Her case is still under investigation."

A tape-recorded message from President Girlie Chichi Vda. de Almagro was repeatedly played on the radio until the crack of dawn: "My people, the adventure of Mr. Art Chavezcu was too good to be true. He has his own virtues and he has his own flaws. He should be admired for his sense of patriotism and his wisdom as a constitutionalist even if his ideas of national sovereignty are impractical when our survival as a democratic nation is at stake. He can dream that he is president, why not? We live in a free country. I happen to be in power and he is not. So we must cast aside his juvenile pretensions and start acting as adults in this deeply Christian nation. United we stand, divided we fall."

In his monastery room, Father Tiburron had been up all night, nervously keeping tab on the live coverage of the march on television until the blackout rendered everything around him in total darkness.

But when it became crystal clear that the attempted coup against the Girlie regime had fizzled out, Father Tiburron jumped out of bed and pounded his chest with clenched fists. Now he could breathe a sigh of relief. The abortive coup attempt was a triumph not only for the Girlie government but for himself. It gave him the upper hand in his crusade to purge his community of Hugo loyalist sentiments. He kept running in his mind the altercation he had with Father Morán in front of their brothers in the religious life — his *mere* subordinates! — where the younger friar had openly challenged and even mocked him.

As he opened the window to allow some breeze from Azucar Bay, he mumbled to himself: "I'll get him in the end. Every dog has its day."

# CHAPTER XII

# Nuncamuere

*And the light shineth in darkness; and the darkness comprehended it not* (John 1:5).

EVERY MORNING WHEN HE wakes up, the first thing Father José Morán does is give thanks to God that he is still alive. Then he does some calisthenics and drinks a glass of water mixed with some drops of lemon fresh from the orchard. After a quick shower, he goes to the only window of his room, parts the curtains and rolls up the blinds for the sea breeze to come in.

He remembers everything like a child who refuses to part with his new pair of shoes, carefully keeping an eye on them to the extent of sleeping with them until a sense of security firms up his Achilles' heel. Or like a soccer player who successfully kicks his first goal toward a multi-million dollar contract in the big league. Or like a poet who unlocks for the first time the nuances of words and, once familiar with the ways of vowels and consonants, make them spring to life.

Remembering is its own reward. Past becomes present, present becomes future. The future reaches out to the past so they both may be one with the present. As the friar surveys his room, getting himself used to its elegant furniture that compliment a bed especially designed for a good night sleep after a weary day, he blinks his eyes a couple of times to get convinced of the present, that at this very moment, he is indeed alive, very much alive, here and now... in Nuncamuere.

Time stands still for the friar. Memories of the past — simple, imperfect, perfect, pluperfect — converge slowly but surely to be absorbed by the present, like the Italian business establishments in Manhattan's Little Italy gobbled up by Chinatown's steady encroachment over the years. The process of remembering reactivates the senses. Memories assault the cranium of his brain with images so clear and so vivid they are embedded in his mind forever the way terror attacks can demolish façades of invincibility or seaquakes can trigger a *tsunami* or a full-scale chemical warfare can foreshadow the Apocalypse.

During their first meeting, President Pacifico Hugo urges Father Morán, in the presence of Roy Gernale, the Hugo loyalist who brings him along to Nuncamuere, to be very vigilant at all times, so that he may never ever lose his vocation. Not even their exile, he stresses, should extinguish the flame of his vocation. He is there solely for spiritual purposes. Only a true servant of God, the President says, can really muster enough guts to care for their souls under the given circumstances. "It's the Judas priests who should be out, Father, not priests like you. God has called and chosen you, and now you are sent to live among his exiles. We are also God's children. You owe it to God to help us keep our faith."

President Hugo then humbly extends his invitation to Roy, to the doctor, to the nurses, to the First Lady and to all those present to join him in praying for the well-being of the friar as well as for the preservation of his priestly ministry.

"Dearest God, are you still there?" the President softly asks, with bowed head and choked with emotions. He then observes a few moments of unbreakable silence. After a seemingly painful, tortured pause, he lifts up his head and, with eyes closed, intones in his signature deep baritone voice: "We beg you, God of all our graces, to incline your ear to all of us repentant sinners: Heavenly Father, thank you so much for sending us a fellow sinner, your priest Father José Morán. We know you love us so much. It is because of this love for us that you allow us to share your Calvary. We have fallen short of human expectations, but we know that your divine love, mercy and forgiveness surpass human understanding. We cling to you, Lord our God, for you are our last refuge. Let every trial we face strengthen our faith. Let every resolve we make be for your greater glory. We, ask you, Lord, to fill Father José Morán with your Holy Spirit so he may do what you want him to do. Give him the courage, the understanding and the patience he needs while ministering to us. Give him the peace of mind he deserves and the sense of fulfillment he seeks. Show your most holy face beneath our sufferings so that his ministry may sanctify those he serves. Keep our faith growing, that we may accept him as we your messenger. Amen."

Roy, who has somewhat lost his faith in the Church because of what some members of the clergy have done to the Hugos — usurping their positions, robbing them of their possessions, stripping them of their sacred honor, labeling them less than humans and refusing to bless them when they die — lights a cigarette and goes to the lanai, ostensibly to smoke.

⁂

He cannot believe that President Hugo, perceived by his political adversaries as the "personification of evil" and coveted by them for his so-called hidden wealth, can pray like a pious little child. But that is what he is, so let him be. He is leaving tomorrow morning anyway. After the cock crows, he is leaving Nuncamuere. Father Morán stays behind.

The friar discusses with the exiled First Couple his schedule of ministering to them. The First Lady mostly does the talking and the two men generally agree with most of her proposals. She is the one running the household anyway and she is familiar with the daily habits of the President and she knows by heart the schedule for his daily medical checkup. They all agree that before six o'clock in the evening, Father Morán leads the Novena followed by the recitation of the Angelus after which he says Mass. Dinner is served after the Mass.

"All right, Father," President Hugo rises, "welcome to Nuncamuere."

⁂

The First Lady invites Roy and Father Morán to stay for an open-air dinner with supporters who come all the way from Islas e Islotes to pledge their unconditional support to the exiled President.

Eighteen round tables covered with red tablecloths and

laden with chocolate bars, nuts, fruit, decorative shells and thank-you cards that serve as centerpieces are impeccably set, evenly distributed at various points of the lawn carpeted with manicured Bermuda grass. Easily accessible from any point of the garden is a long table wrapped in red, white and blue tablecloths where a roasted suckling pig and other catered food are laid. The well-lighted oak tree near the gazebo is tied with red ribbons and decorated with flaglets of Islas e Islotes, and underneath it a hind quarter of beef is being roasted.

Father Morán is requested to bless the food. "He is a man of God," Luz de los Cielos, scheduled to go back to Islas e Islotes at the end of the month, announces. "Father will bless the food."

"A Hugo loyalist priest," an aghast, crop-haired blonde male in his late twenties verbalizes his disbelief. Turning to his companion, a fortyish-looking short-haired woman, he asks her in a very soft, very feminine voice: "Do you have a pen?"

The woman gives him what he is asking for.

It is the idea of the friar not to wear the habit or the Roman collar while in Nuncamuere. He wears the alb and the chasuble at Mass. Outside, he mingles with the people in civilian clothes.

"*Deus qui foecit totum*," Father Morán blesses the food, "*benedicat coebum et potum.*"

"That's Latin," the blonde man, limply gesticulating with his wrist, tells in very soft, very feminine voice the woman who just growls like a wrestler in response.

While the others have joined the beeline to get their share of dinner, the two linger on their chairs. Father Morán steals a glance at them in time to see them surreptitiously putting chocolate bars inside the signature handbag of the woman.

"Ma'am," he overhears Luz de los Cielos telling the First Lady, "they ridicule you. They call you imeldific. They say you have surpassed Marie Antoinette in ostentatious extravagance. By the way, the mother pearls on your ears look priceless. I have never seen one as big as those before. You look so elegant in your dress. Beside you I certainly look like a beggar, especially now that they have taken away my job to silence me and prevent me from calling you the most beautiful First Lady in the universe."

"Sweetheart," the First Lady chuckles, "I bought them this morning at the thrift shop for five dollars. This dress cost me eight dollars."

Dulzura Zetineb, porcelain-complexioned sister of Julio Zetineb, escorted by a punk half her age goes to the table of the President and gives him a buss. She nods at the punk and he hands over to the aide of the President a big manila envelope. She supports the Hugo loyalists movement, she explains in her hardly audible genteel voice, and she wants to be reimbursed for her expenses. Father Morán does not want to overhear anything more of her stories, so he excuses himself and heads for the bathroom.

The friar steps on an object. He bends down to examine what it is and is stunned to find an earring of glowing solid white gold encrusted with sparkling emeralds, rubies and diamonds.

Just then, the bathroom door opens and an overweight, overdressed woman waddles her way out. "That's mine!" she snaps, snatching the ring from the friar with the determination of a greedy child fighting for her most prized position. She steps on a banana peeling on her way back to her table, falling flat on her back with a thud. The noise she has created alerts two members of the kitchen staff who promptly come running to help her up.

The friar opens the bathroom, but quickly steps back. The woman has not bothered to flush the toilet after using it. Upon realizing that he does not need the bathroom after all, he decides to go back by way of the bar where the catering staff are mixing the drinks.

"Dulzura is as greedy as her brother," the source of the voice sounds all too familiar. He is right. It is Jessie, the law student supposed to have been arrested for being one of the ringleaders of the Hugo Forever freedom marchers. He observes Jessie spitting into two glasses of soda.

"Give this to Dulzura," Jessie instructs a waitress who appears to be enjoying her mission. "She deserves my sputum," Jessie tells the waitress who is obviously in connivance with him. "And this one to her boy toy. They have not spent anything for the loyalists. She claims she is here to sympathize with the Hugos, but she and her boy toy are here as freeloaders. They want their expenses to be reimbursed? Vultures!"

By the time Father Morán goes back to his table, dinner is in progress. It is a picture perfect evening for an outdoor dinner. The moon is full. There are no clouds in the sky that becomes a star-studded dome for mortals who find respite, no matter how fleeting, in this gathering where they can freely exercise their right to be human.

Singer Melinda Solis starts belting out "I Shall Return," and all eyes are focused on President Hugo. Those present are looking for any clue from every gesture of the exiled President that may indicate that he is indeed returning to Islas e Islotes.

Luz de los Cielos waves the V-sign and on cue the diners burst into a subdued chant of *"Hu-go! Hu-go! Hu-go forever!"*

Roy softly taps the shoulder of Father Morán. The First Lady wants to discuss something very confidential with both of them.

The First Lady finds the friar very naïve looking and guileless. Nobody will ever suspect him of committing any indiscretions. "Perfect!" she exclaims, looking at Roger.

"Ahem..." Roy stammers. "Ma'am wants you to look for money...."

"No problem," the friar responds. "I can ask my friends to give donation to the exiled President..."

"No need for that. You can be the carrier."

"You mean of money?"

"Something like that. Call it funds."

"I have to be honest with you," the friar flatly answers. "Anything but money. Money can give you anything except happiness; it can bring you anywhere except to heaven."

Luz de los Cielos is now calling the First Lady to sing. "By public demand," she says. "Most beautiful First Lady of the universe, you must comply!"

The First Lady sings "Maite," a Basque song, in its Spanish version. *"Lejos de aquel instante...Lejos de aquel lugar...A un corazón amante...Siento resuscitar...Vuelve su imagen bella... En mi memoria a ver...Como un fulgur de estrellas...Muerto al amanecer..."*

The crowd, especially the President, is electrified. A swath of silence paralyzes the evening air and leads the mind into the attic of remembering, bitter and sweet but most sweet as they behold her, enabling their capacity to admire, to hero worship, and her face makes everybody fall in love with her and for them she can do no wrong even if she claims to be the mother of her country where only a handful of oligarchs rule and the rest live no better than serfs as in the last days of Marie Antoinette. Nostalgia, emptiness and loneliness caress the heart of everyone, making them pine for the not-so-distant past when her face was all over, but now that past seems to have frozen into the abstraction of the good, the true and the beautiful, incomprehensible and unsustainable, and they are hurled back to earth again, like the mythical Icarus falling headlong into the sea, his waxen wings melted for flying too close to the sun.

A loud banging upon the main gate awakens them from their incursion into what could have been's and if only's.

"The police!" one of the Gringolander security guards on duty reports to the President."

"Let them come in," the President calmly replies.

"No need," another Gringolander security guard on duty tells the President. "They just want her to stop singing. The neighbors are complaining. They just want her to stop singing."

The common question embedded in everybody's mind is: Why are the security guards all Gringolanders? And yet everybody prefers to remain silent. The mind retreats into a sphinx-like, I-don't-care attitude. Silence becomes the better part of valor.

"They don't even want me to sing," the First Lady laments. "They want to sequester all my rights as a human being, including my right to sing."

All the crowd can do is look up at the sky dome studded with stars above them, and go back to their separate lives with a collective sigh of helplessness. The helplessness of the exiled.

"There's a laptop and a desktop for your personal use," Siegfrid tells the friar as he gives him a tour of the chalet. "The gym's in the basement. This place is electronically protected. You are number 1. I am number 2. When you ring the doorbell, ring once. If you hear the doorbell sounding twice, it's me. Here's the key to the hideaway. Don't be too curious."

Roy, for his part, is all set to go to Glendale. The plane leaves at ten o'clock in the morning and he plans to check in three hours earlier. He travels light, but he wants to be early. He needs to buy some presents for his son Rio and his brother-in-law Lorenzo.

Roy hands him an unused wallet with some dollar bills and a calling card where his email address and his mobile telephone number are printed. He is visiting California to see how his son Rio is faring in his studies. Río stays with his mother Corina's younger brother. He is enrolled in a computer course in Glendale.

⁂

The freedom march of the Hugo loyalists ended up in their violent dispersal by the pink army. The marchers were prevented from reaching the capital. Those perceived to be ring leaders were placed under arrest. Roy's eldest son, Andoy, was among the unlucky ones who perished.

Father Morán is still in limbo on how Jessie has managed to escape and relocate to Nuncamuere, but he keeps it to himself.

Luckily for the family of Father Morán, they had been spirited away by both Lieutenant Evans Marfori and Ganymede and deposited in a safehouse a couple of days before the bloody melee. Ganymede took his mother Eva, who was not with the freedom marchers, out of their rented apartelle. She stayed for the time being in the apartment of Lieutenant Marfori, disguised as a cook and washerwoman. As for Ganymede, Roy Gernale has not forgotten his voluntary commitment to Father Morán. He hired Ganymede to collect rent for his apartment buildings at the university belt. Ganymede occupied one of the apartments to make it easier for his life as a university student.

⁂

With Roy Gernale gone, Father José Morán is now on his own in Nuncamuere. His only companion in the chalet is Siegfrid. Now he is all alone by himself. Siegfrid is out to procure their grocery needs.

The chalet is well landscaped with different kinds of flowers, cacti, potted petunias, ivies, buttercups and a separate herbal garden. A gazebo made entirely of seashells, surrounded by grapefruit and lemon trees, is situated at a good vantage point where one can get a glimpse of the Atlantic Ocean to the left and an ample view of a golf course to the right. Occasionally mongooses dash by in lightning speed, a clue that there are no snakes around.

Father Morán randomly opens the Bible and silently reads Mark 3:1-6: "And he entered again into the synagogue; and there was a man there which had a withered hand. And they watched him, whether he would heal him on the sabbath day; that they might accuse him. And he said unto the man which had the withered hand, Stand forth. And he said unto them, Is it lawful to do good on the sabbath days, or to do evil? to save life, or to kill? But they held their peace. And when he had looked round about on them with anger, being grieved for the hardness of their hearts, he said unto the man, Stretch forth your hand. And he stretched it out: and his hand was restored whole as the other. And the Pharisees went forth, and straightway took counsel with the Herodians against him, how they might destroy him."

The friar closes the Bible and reflects on the passages he has just read for a good ten minutes. He then reaches for his journal, puts it on top of a working table, pulls a chair and starts writing:

"I will let no day pass without writing a single line. Whether I will survive this crisis in my life or not does not matter anymore. In Chinese writing, crisis and opportunity are both represented by one single character. I treat this crisis, and every crisis for that matter, as an opportunity to discover my limitations, to overcome my fears, to firmly put my feet on the ground, to face reality...to better survive. Clericalism, careerism, simony and ruthless opportunism have festered the bowels of the church like cancer. So many people have either canceled their faith or switched religion.

"I am in Nuncamuere to minister to the exiled First Family. Priests and bishops, past frequent visitors of the Hugos, are nowhere to be seen. The pastor and the local priests are not allowed by the bishop to say Mass for the Hugos.

"God is my boss. He knows how to take care of me. I am a priest of Jesus Christ, the Son of God made Man who has come into this world 'to preach the Gospel to the poor; to heal the brokenhearted, to preach deliverance to the captives, and recovering of sight to the blind, to set at liberty them that are bruised.'"

The friar closes the journal and makes the sign of the cross. He places the Bible on top of the bedside table and goes back to the window.

It is a beautiful morning. The sun is up and shining and the irises are in bloom. Butterflies flutter from buttercups to hibiscus while dragonflies nosedive like miniature airplanes. Three birds of paradise frolic on the manicured lawn.

He pumps more air into his lungs by inhaling deeply to jump start his breathing exercise. The doorbell rings twice. Siegfrid is back. He helps him unload the groceries and put them in the pantry and the refrigerator. They hurriedly set the table. A few minutes later they are bantering over breakfast of yogurt, grapes, cheese and kiwi fruits. Siegfrid makes his own coffee and mixes a shake of fresh goat's milk.

❧

"Lovely *señorita...*" The boy José can hardly keep pace with his Grandpa Eliodoro's long strides. Every day, at sunrise, Grandpa Eliodoro makes a routine inspection of their sugarcane plantation.

These are his happiest years. The names of Grandpa Eliodoro and of Grandma Francisca command reverence in the whole village. They are on everybody's lips because of their goodwill and generosity. Anyone in need who comes to their house never leaves empty-handed. Such a generosity is part and parcel of their faith based on their Bible Baptist religion.

Today is Saturday, and José walks with his Grandpa Eliodoro. The boy stays with his grandparents for the weekend so he can attend, together with other children his age, the Sunday school conducted by the Baptist missionaries under the pergola. They are given a breakfast of pancakes, hot chocolate and fruits. During recess they are served popcorn. Before dismissal, every child attendee is provided with school supplies and coloring books.

"Lovely *Señorita....*" Grandpa Eliodoro repeats the phrase, this time in an off-key sing-song voice.

José smiles and looks up at his Grandpa Eliodoro. His Grandpa Eliodoro does not need to sing because he can paint. For him, his Grandpa Eliodoro is the greatest. He wants to be like his Grandpa Eliodoro when he grows up. He will paint Tinin-awan sunset and Mampunay at noon. The former is his Grandpa Eliodoro's vast sugarcane *hacienda* while the latter is his grandpa's coffee plantation. He will paint all lovely *señoritas* he meets. Just like what his Grandpa Eliodoro does.

His Grandpa Eliodoro and his Grandma Francisca dot on him. When a consequential visitor comes around, his Grandpa Eliodoro calls him and introduces him as his "budding apprentice." He has his materials ready all the time. He has no difficulty sketching any visitor.

"Will you give the *Lovely Señorita* to me, Grandpa Eliodoro?" he asks.

"Yes, of course. You can already draw a horse. Your granny showed your drawing to me. When one day you happen to meet a lovely *señorita* you love, paint her, too."

"I've found her already!"

"Is her name Miriam?" his Grandpa Eliodoro teases him. Miriam is a long-legged girl who can outrun anybody and can box like her uncle Little Dado, the village pugilist.

"No! I've not met her in person yet."

"Who is she that I may help you paint her? Where does she live?"

"She is the Dutch Girl."

"But that's one of my silhouettes," Eliodoro chuckles.

Dutch Girl is the brand name of his grandson's favorite milk, so Grandpa Eliodoro has made a silhouette called "Dutch Girl" and has given it to him during his sixth birthday. Once, Grandpa Eliodoro remembers, José is asked by one of the Sunday school teachers what he wants to do when he grows up. The boy answers: "Marry the Dutch Girl."

"How practical!" his Grandma Francisca gives his response a high mark. "He's not like his cousin Seneca who spends the rest of the day crying when they cannot give him Mount Kanlaon for breakfast."

As a high school freshman, José Morán is able to uncork the genie of poetry within him just waiting to be released.

Their English teacher, a young glamorous lady, brings to class a calendar, each illustrated with a picture of a beautiful spot on earth to visit. "You can select any month and any picture for you to write about," she instructs them. "Do not write your name. If I read your work tomorrow, that means you have the making of a writer."

The following day, the teacher reads "Yosemite Valley." She then looks at her student one by one and pronounces her verdict: "Whoever wrote this piece has the making of a writer. Who's the author of this piece? Raise your right hand."

José raises his right hand. All eyes are suddenly focused on him and his face turns red. He feels a bit awkward and clumsy but nevertheless satisfied with the teacher's judgment.

The teacher cannot conceal her admiration. She proceeds with the class and then starts reading some verses. They are what she calls "limericks."

"Limericks," she lectures, "are nonsensical poems of five lines; the first, second and fifth lines rhyming, and the third line rhyming with the fourth. I want all of you to write five limericks. Submit them to me on Monday. You have the whole weekend to do your assignment. I will read the three best limericks on Friday. And don't write your name there or give a clue in any way about your identity."

Friday comes and the teacher reads not three but five best limericks. "They are all so good," she tells her class. "I cannot decide which are the best three. These five are the best limericks ever written by my students. Could the authors of these limericks please stand?"

José is the author of what, according to their teacher, are the five best limericks written by her students.

Father Morán opens the laptop and the desktop one after another. They look new but they are already configured, ready to be used. He installs Skype in both computers and opens an account for each one. He opens his email and sends Roy a message with the complete text of the Prayer to Saint Michael the Archangel which he has the habit of praying daily before he leaves his room. "O glorious prince Saint Michael, chief and commander of the heavenly hosts, guardian of souls, vanquisher of rebel spirits, servant in the house of the Divine King and our admirable conductor, you who shine with excellence and superhuman virtue, deliver us from all evil who turn to you with confidence and enable us by your gracious protection to serve God more and more faithfully every day. Amen."

For Río, he makes an attachment of the Daily Prayer to Guardian Angel: "Angel of God, my guardian dear, to whom God's love commits me here, ever this day be at my side to light and guard, to rule and guide. Amen."

Deep in his heart, Father Morán knows that his vocation is a real calling. He does not only believe it, he knows it with moral certainty. Sometimes his priestly vocation has been placed in jeopardy, due in part to his lack of malice and innate naiveté, but he remains steadfast in his knowledge

that he has been called to serve God to make the world a
better place.

He can easily attract attention wherever he is without
intending it. He does not use their community car because
he cannot drive. Father Tiburron has arrogated unto himself
the exclusive use of the car. Father Morán uses public trans-
portation. Or walks.

One afternoon, while Father Tiburron is demonstrating
to the pious ladies how efficient he is in driving in total con-
trast to Father Morán who knows no better, a BMW pulls
up at the church patio. A uniformed driver emerges from the
car and goes straight to Father Tiburron to ask for Father
Morán. He is being sought by his granduncle, a cousin of
his late Grandpa Eliodoro, an alleged Hugo "crony." After
that incident, Father Morán is mocked behind his back by
Father Tiburron.

So you are *the* Father José Morán?" He finds something odd
in the way the question is phrased, but the friar assumes that
the guy seated on the other bed inside his hotel room is trying
hard to sound clever, so he answers: "And you are..."

"Just call me Lud. I've been observing you all the while,"
the man tells him. "You do not seem to be what someone
has been brainwashing me about you. You do know Father
Derovere Tiburron, don't you?"

"We are brothers in the cassock. You must be his friend?"

"He loves to portray himself as my friend. He is an ac-
quaintance, never a friend. Never has been, never is, never
will be. That brother in the cassock of yours is a real pest, a

poseur, a fraud. He forces himself on us and extorts money from us in God's name. We call him 'The Extortionist.' He desperately wants to join our tour to Tibet. He expects to be paid for doing nothing. Who wants him anyways? He's ignorant and arrogant. He lacks social graces and he's a dud. Be prepared. He is up to something with some human rights violators in the military. At the mere mention of your name, he badmouths you."

They are in Lhasa, Tibet, inside the hotel room assigned to him. The friar has been invited by travel editors and businessmen to join them in Lhasa. He is not there as a chaplain but as a friend.

It has been decided that a single room be reserved for the friar and the rest can share a room, each with two occupants. The friar accommodates Lud to occupy the extra bed in his room for a night because he arrives late and there has been a mix-up in the room assignment.

The hotel management runs out of oxygen tanks. Almost everyone has difficulty breathing. "We are at the roof of the world," Lud says. "As you know, it's winter in Chengdu."

"Yes, it's winter," the friar agrees, "but why is the air-conditioner on?"

He makes a motion to turn off the air-conditioner, only to realize that the unit is centralized. He picks up the intercom and dials the number of the manager.

"He's not around," a woman's voice responds.

"We don't need any air-conditioner, we need a heater," the friar calmly responds.

In less than ten minutes, the problem is fixed. The group decides to stay for a week.

Lud feels guilty and awful. He is one of those enjoying the tidbits offered by Father Tiburron to some gullible wealthy Chinese businessmen like him concerning the idiosyncrasies of Father José Morán. "In poetry," Lud tells them, "Father Morán is a giant. But in practical things in life, he is a fetus."

"Where are you going?" The friar asks Lud as the man opens the door, mobile phone in his hand.

"I'll call Father Tiburron now," Lud tells the friar. I'll tell him you are with us."

"Good. Tell him, so far, so good."

Lud does not want to tell Father Morán that he wants Father Tiburrón to have sleepless nights out of envy or jealousy or both. That slanderer of his fellow friar can eat his heart out.

⊰⊱

When it rains in Nuncamuere, it pours. At first it is only a drizzle but before one can yawn, it has become a heavy downpour.

Seated before the laptop, Father Morán reaches for his journal, opens it, and attempts scribbling some lines. It takes him some time to gather his thoughts, but he forces himself to write just about anything that comes to mind at this very moment.

"Everything seems to be fine with me. Everything seems to be okay with me. I live for the day. In any case, that in itself is everything to write about.

"I neither look back nor look ahead. I just look at today. Day after day, today well lived is forever. Today is tomorrow and tomorrow is today.

"Today, I receive an email from Peter John. He is doing very well in his line of work. He is now married and his son is in college.

"Today I come across the blog of Roger Dean. His poems that he posts there under a pseudonym are breathtaking. He has left the ministry and is now happily married with an ex-nun, a former formator of her congregation. She has two Ph.Ds. Their son has just graduated with honors. They have an accredited school. Roger has composed the alma mater song of their school.

"Today I chat on Skype with Father Trinity. He has been appointed pastor of a parish in Perth. He takes possession of his parish today.

"It does not snow in Nuncamuere. But it does rain. Outside it is raining heavily as I write this."

The friar closes his journal, goes to the bedside table and opens his laptop. After making the sign of the cross, he starts typing: "Imeldific, End Times Fairy Tale."